TOREL

Star-Crossed Alien Mail Order Brides

SUSAN HAYES

ABOUT THE BOOK

What do you do when your planet runs out of women? Send for takeout, of course.

Torel is the best medical officer in the Pyrosian fleet, but being the best comes with a cost. When the queen orders him to apply to Star-Crossed Dating, he's relieved when there's no match for him among the human females of Earth. He doesn't have time for that kind of distraction.

Mated or not, he's on his way to Earth to help newly-mated females adjust to the life awaiting them on Pyros. All he has to do is keep them healthy and happy during the voyage home. It should be the easiest assignment of his career.

This book contains a widow determined to never fall in

love again, and a doctor who is about to discover that when it comes to the heart, he's still got a lot to learn.

SUSAN HAYES

ALL RIGHTS RESERVED: This literary work may not be reproduced or transmitted in any form or by any means, including electronic or photographic reproduction, in whole or in part, without express written permission.

All characters and events in this book are fictitious. Any resemblance to actual persons living or dead is strictly coincidental. It is fiction so facts and events may not be accurate except to the current world the book takes place in.

Copyright © 2018 Susan Hayes

Torel (Book #5 of the Star-crossed Alien Mail Order Brides Series)

First E-book Publication: October 2018

Cover Design: crocodesigns.com

Editor: Dayna Hart

Published by: Black Scroll Publications

ISBN: 978-1-988446-33-2

CHAPTER ONE

HALEY DUCKED around a corner and then peeked back the way they'd come. It wasn't an ideal vantage point, but sports arenas weren't exactly designed with covert observation in mind. "Do you think she'll be okay?"

Piper nodded, her gaze fixed on her older sister, Aria. "Now that she's through the gate, yeah. I think so. I really hope she doesn't turn her match down before she gives him a chance, though."

"Me too," Haley agreed. "She's one of the kindest women I've ever known. I'd like to see her happy, even if it means she ends up on another planet." Aria had once been Haley's grief counsellor, but over time, their relationship had changed to a friendship. Losing Jeff to cancer had shattered Haley's world. Aria had been her rock through those stormy times, and now she was the only real friend Haley had.

Piper sighed and swept a stray lock of her bright blue hair out of her face. "I'm afraid that's one of the reasons she plans to turn him down. She doesn't want to leave us."

"I know." Haley weighed her next words carefully. "Would you be okay if she did go?"

Piper shot her a look of pure frustration. "Of course I'll be okay. I love my sister, but she needs to cut the apron string and focus on her life instead of mine."

"She worries about you, Pi."

"I know. And I know it comes from a place of love and all that, but I'm an adult. Have been for years. When is she going to stop mothering me?"

Haley patted the younger woman's shoulder. "How does never sound? Because even if she winds up on the far side of the galaxy, you know she's going to find a way to keep tabs on us both. Caring about others is Aria's superpower."

Piper nodded and glanced around the corner again. "She's headed inside. Guess this means we should go find our seats, huh? I hope we've got a good view. I know I didn't get matched, but that doesn't mean I can't enjoy the scenery."

"I'm planning on enjoying the view, too. I don't want a match, but I wouldn't mind taking home one of those alien hotties for a few days."

The two of them followed the mostly female crowd through the corridors, keeping an eye out for signs pointing to their seating area. "You ever think you'll want more than a few days of fun with a guy?"

"Nope. I found the perfect guy once, and then I lost him to cancer. I can't go through that again. I'm a solo act from now on." You only got one chance at a love like that. The thought of dating again made her want to curl into a ball and hide.

"So that's it? You're done?"

"I'm not done with men, no. I just don't want to keep them. I'm sticking with the catch and release approach from now on."

Piper didn't comment until they had descended a flight of stairs and found their row. "I'm not sure I want that. I used to, but lately…"

Haley did a careful sidestep along the narrow space between the seats and questioned her choice to wear her new Prada heels today. They were gorgeous, but not exactly practical. "You're almost out of your twenties. It's not surprising you're starting to think longer term. I was a little older than you when I realized that I wanted more."

"That's why I took a chance with the Star-Crossed dating thing. It didn't work out, though."

"There's an entire planet of men looking for mates. Don't give up, yet." She sat down and scanned the scene in front of her. The domed roof of BC Place was open, allowing the summer sun to fill the space with light. In the middle of the dome was a large, white, elegantly-decorated tent. Sitting beneath it were a large group of women, all dressed up and clearly nervous. None of them could keep still for long, and even from their elevated seats, she could hear their high-pitched voices as they chatted with each other.

"Good point." Piper sat down beside her and tossed

her bag into the empty seat to her left. "Do you think they have firefighters on their planet? I should probably date one in case the next place I get a job catches fire, too."

Haley winked at Piper. "Best fire insurance a girl can have. Those guys really know how to handle their hoses."

"Oh my god, I cannot believe you said that out loud. And my sister is worried *I'm* going to be a bad influence on Melody." Piper was still laughing as she leaned forward in her chair and looked down at the arena floor. "Do you see Aria?"

"Near the front of the tent, looking like she's going to bolt at any second."

"She's not the only one who looks like they're having second thoughts. Me, I'd be admiring the scenery already on display." Piper pointed to where several tall, broad-shouldered men were standing at the edge of the stage set up at one end of the arena.

The girl wasn't wrong about the view. Haley took a moment to appreciate it for herself. It was the first time she had seen a Pyrosian in person, and the pictures she had seen didn't do them justice. She pulled out her phone, captured a few pictures of the aliens, and then continued taking pictures of the rest of the arena. Officially, she was here as a friend, but that didn't mean she couldn't take pictures and observe as much as she could.

There was a story here, she just wasn't sure what form it would take, yet. Everything seemed to be on the up-and-up, but any journalist worth her words knew looks could be deceiving. The best stories were always buried deeper. Aria was here because she'd made a simple misclick and accepted a match with an alien. She hadn't intended to do it, but there had been no undo button. Were the Pyrosians playing fair, or were there other women here who had been tricked into coming to meet their matches?

No one knew much about how the first human women had met their mates, either. Oh, sure, Haley had seen the promotional materials and ads that were all over television and the internet. There probably wasn't a human on the planet who hadn't at this point, but ads and copy didn't tell the truth, they crafted a message.

If she thought there was something truly nefarious going on, she would never have encouraged Aria to come here today. It wasn't that she thought the Pyrosians were plotting the demise of humanity or anything, but everyone had secrets…and if she kept her eyes open, maybe she could uncover one or two of them.

Her father was constantly demanding she prove herself to him. What better way to do that than to get the scoop of a lifetime about the first alien race to visit Earth? She was a good reporter, even if it wasn't her dream job. All her dreams had died with Jeff.

Several more men appeared to one side of the stage. One was pale blond, the other had dark hair, and they were both wearing what looked like designer suits. They were accompanied by several serious-looking soldiers wearing dark uniforms, and it was obvious they were there to protect the new arrivals. These must be VIP's, and apparently they knew how to dress for success here on Earth.

A blonde woman in a flowing sundress of orange and yellow joined them a minute later. She walked right through the guards and up to the dark-haired Pyrosian, kissing his cheek with obvious affection. It was hard to be sure, given the distance, but Haley thought the woman was human. In fact, she looked kind of familiar.

"Is that one of the women from the ads?" Piper asked.

Of course. "I think so, yeah. So the guy she just smooched must be her mate."

"Too bad he's taken, he's easy on the eyes. Then again, so is that platinum-blond hottie beside him."

Haley raised her phone and used the camera to zoom in on the group just as they turned to greet another group of VIP's, this one followed by a camera crew. "Looks like the mayor has arrived."

"Must be getting close to showtime, then," Piper replied.

Haley took a few more photos and then used her phone to zoom in Aria. She seemed alright, though she was still nervous. She thought about sending her a text message to let her know she wasn't alone, but Aria had her hands full keeping Melody entertained and happy, so she decided against it.

When she looked back at the stage, things had changed. The crowd of VIP's had grown, and they were taking their seats in a roped-off area to the right of the main stage. There were more uniformed Pyrosians appearing now, and plenty of organizers running around, checking in with each other and then dashing off again.

It wasn't long before everyone and everything seemed to be in place. The Pyrosian soldiers were lined up in formation on each side of the stage, the guests were all seated, and a low chorus of gasps filled the arena as a ship descended out of the sky and through the open roof of the stadium. At the same time, more Pyrosians started filing onto the stadium floor. They were all men, all in matching outfits, and Haley guessed they must be the ones who had been matched to the lucky women awaiting them under the tent.

There were feminine murmurs of approval from all over the arena as they marched toward their places. As entrances went, it was damned impressive – until the explosion.

TOREL ZINN HAD WORKED hard to become the head medical officer for the Pyrosian royal family. One of the benefits of his position was being able to attend to members of the family while they were aboard the fleet's flagship, the *Firebrand*. That had allowed him to be present when the first human females were brought on board and given him the chance to watch his friend and commander fall for his human mate, Gwen.

Now, they were in orbit around Earth for the second time. He should be preparing for the arrival of the newly claimed human females assigned to the ship, but instead, he was sitting behind his desk, across from one of the richest males in the galaxy.

"You should come down with us, Torel. I'm taking my mate back to the sea wall where she used to work. It's a pretty spot--nice views, lots of people, and fresh air. Then, Lisa wants to introduce me to something called poutine. Fried carbohydrates smothered in meaty gravy and cheese. We're having it for lunch before heading to the stadium. You're welcome to join us. In fact, it might be handy to have a doctor on hand, just in case this food doesn't agree with Pyrosian biology. What do you say? Want to stress-test your heart?" Vadir asked, his golden eyes gleaming with an alarming level of amusement.

When Vadir was this happy, he was usually up to something. Often, it was something bordering on illegal. Vadir had enough money, charm, and power to talk himself out of any trouble. Torel didn't. "Thanks for the offer, but I've been invited to join the Prince and Princess on their shuttle. I'll see you at the ceremony, and I'll make sure to bring something for an upset stomach, just in case."

"Got anything that might help a Romaki's digestion?" Vadir asked casually.

"Why would I need...." Torel stared at Vadir with dawning alarm. "By the Flames of the First Ones, what have you done? Romaki dragons haven't left their homeworld for hundreds of years. Why would I need to treat one?"

Vadir winked and leaned back in his chair. "One dragon did. He's been staying out of sight on my ship since we met up with the *Firebrand*. And before you ask, yes, Joran knows he's here. We've been keeping it quiet, obviously, but he's attending the ceremony as my guest."

Well, that explained why Vadir looked so happy. He was about to introduce humanity to yet-another alien species. No doubt he'd be doing all he could to broker more trade deals between the three planets during this visit.

"Do his leaders know he's here? What if he's injured? No one knows much about treating a Romaki. There's no need-- since they're bound by law not to leave the planet."

"He's a *dragon*. There isn't a weapon on Earth that could hurt him. Relax, Torel. He's my responsibility, not yours. And no, his parents don't know he's here."

"Parents?" Torel asked, already thankful that whatever Vadir said next, it wasn't his responsibility to deal with it.

"My guest is Prince Radek, youngest son of the rulers of the Romaki Snow Dragon clan."

"Has anyone ever mentioned you're a lunatic with the ethics of starving *paka*?"

Vadir laughed. "It's been mentioned once or twice." He rose from his chair and walked around Torel's small office to clasp his shoulder in a firm grip. "I appreciate you making time to see me today, with everything that's going on."

"Always. You're about to become a father for the first time, and your baby will have parents from two different species. Questions and concerns are to be expected. Anything you or Lisa need, you are always welcome to speak with me." He might never have children of his own, but Torel took great pride in knowing the royal family had expanded his duties to include overseeing the pregnancy and eventual delivery of every child with a human mother. He would train others as plans progressed, but for now, he was the one everyone would come to.

Vadir said his goodbyes and departed, leaving Torel alone. Soon, he'd be on his way to Earth with the rest of the royal party. This was probably the last time he'd have peace and quiet until they returned to Pyros. The entire ship would shortly be full of newly mated couples in the thrall of the Scorching. He was expecting to deal with more than a few injuries, strains, and exhaustion by the time things settled down.

Today was a good day for Pyros. After years of desperate research, they still hadn't determined why so few females were born each generation. Now, they had the human females to help restore the balance. It was a historic moment, and he was pleased to be part of it. He had no time for a mate of his own, but he didn't need a mate and offspring to make his mark. The Gods had provided him another way. His study of the human/Pyrosian matings and their offspring would be his legacy. Though that argument had not stopped the queen from insisting he register as a potential mating partner. Thankfully, there was no match for him in the database. His work was too important to allow anything to distract from it, and a mate would be the greatest distraction he could imagine.

He ran a hand over his bearded jaw. He'd grown the beard while on vacation and kept it because his mother had liked it. "You look tired," she'd told him during their last day together. "Not your body, but your soul. You push yourself too hard. Find something that makes you happy and indulge yourself once in a while. There's more to life than work, Torel. Your father and I are grateful for all you've done for us, and so very proud of you. It's time to take care of yourself."

It was good advice, but he'd spent most of his adult life working toward two goals: excelling in his career and making sure his parents would spend the rest of their lives financially secure. Now he'd achieved those goals, he had no idea how to switch gears. Not that he planned on trying. He knew what he had to do next—ensure his race continued. It would be the work of a lifetime.

A FEW HOURS LATER, Torel was on a shuttle headed to Earth. It was his first visit, and he was curious to experience the place for himself. He'd been studying the planet and its inhabitants for more than a year, but there were some things data couldn't tell him.

The scenery displayed on the wall monitor was breathtaking. The city of Vancouver was nestled between soaring mountains and one of Earth's many oceans, and he had a brief pang of regret he hadn't taken Vadir up on his offer.

The shuttle slowed its descent as they approached the city, and several military craft fell into formation around them. "I didn't know we were getting an honour guard," he said.

Commander Denza glanced over at him and shook his head. "We're not. They're our security escort, assigned by the humans for our protection."

Torel sat up straighter in his chair. "Why do we need protecting? And what do they think their craft can accomplish that ours couldn't do better?"

"Apparently, not all the humans are celebrating our arrival. A small faction has formed decrying our arrival as a threat. They are also opposed to the agreement with their governments allowing us to claim human females as mates. We were only made aware of this issue upon our arrival in orbit." The commander's frown deepened. "If we had known, we would have changed plans, which is why we weren't informed."

"I'm sure it's nothing to worry about, Kash." Maggie, Joran's Earth-born princess, said. "Security was doubled at your request, and almost everyone there today will either be part of the gathering or be hoping for a match of their own someday."

"I still don't like it," Kash grumbled.

"I know you don't, but that's because you take your job seriously." Gwen, another human female, leaned over and kissed her mate on the cheek. "You really need to try and smile, though. You're terrifying when you get all grumpy and fierce, and that's not the message we're going for today."

Torel laughed. "If you want him to smile, just give him Hope to hold. He'll be grinning in seconds."

"And making silly noises, too. I like this idea. It will show the humans we are as devoted to our children as we are to our mates." Joran reached out to take Maggie's hand. "Make that happen, will you, Gwen?"

The banter continued for the next little while, but Torel retreated from the conversation. While he was on friendly terms with everyone present, things had changed since Joran and Kash claimed their mates. It wasn't that he was being deliberately excluded, but he didn't quite feel like he belonged in their circle any longer.

He turned his attention back to the monitor and almost immediately spotted the white dome of the stadium where the Gathering was happening. The shuttle slowed and began its final descent a few seconds later, and he watched as they made straight for the opening at the top of the dome.

An air of anticipation took hold as everyone peered at the monitors.

"Almost home," Maggie said, quietly.

Joran cleared his throat. "That is not your home any longer, my *seska*. You are of Pyros, now."

They were all laughing at her slip when a deafening boom tore through the air. Before he could move, the shuttle started to shake and pitch, throwing him against his safety harness. The cabin filled with grunts and curses as the overhead lights flickered and several more explosions rocked the ship. The shuttle banked hard to the left and started to climb so quickly the inertial dampeners couldn't keep up. The g-forces pressed him down into his seat, and by the time Torel could move again, they were clear of the stadium.

He glanced at the monitor and his stomach twisted. A plume of dark-grey smoke spiraled up out of stadium's open roof. He looked over at Kash, who was already barking orders into his communicator, trying to find out what had happened. Torel pulled out his own communicator and accessed the medical emergency sub-channel. What should have been a joyous occasion had just been transformed into a nightmare. He sent out an alert, notifying the medical officers on every ship to man their posts and dispatch medics to the surface as soon as it was safe to do so. Soon, he'd be back on the *Firebrand*, awaiting the first casualties. Until then, all he could do was prepare and pray for the wounded.

CHAPTER TWO

THE FIRST FEW times Haley roused, it was to a dark world full of jagged pain. Her head felt like it was full of broken glass, and even the slightest movement caused a symphony of agonies. Every time she tried to move or open her eyes, the pain would rise to a crescendo and she'd fall back into the darkness again.

She drifted like that for a long time, fading in and out without ever really waking. Somewhere along the way the pain stopped, but she didn't know when or how. Wakefulness came slowly, and with it came fragments of memories -- brief flashes that played in her head like bits of spliced-together film. The first terrible blast. Terror. Her and Piper, running for one of the exits as the world erupted around them. She'd fallen, twisting an ankle. She remembered Piper yelling at her, telling her to get up and get her shoes off. Running again. Chaos, fear, and then a tap to the back of her head, followed by a long stretch of nothing.

She drifted again, but over time, soft sounds began to intrude on her consciousness, coaxing her to wakefulness. There was something familiar about wherever she was, and it made her uneasy.

I'm not going to figure it out until I open my eyes.

She cracked one eye open. At first, all she saw was white. White walls. White ceiling. Stark and pristine, like a hospital –. Shit, no. She hated hospitals. She'd spent too much time in them watching helplessly as Jeff wasted away. The doctors had done their best, she knew that, but she'd learned to dread their hushed conversations in the corner of the room as they consulted with each other about how best to hold off death a little longer.

Someone appeared in her field of vision. A bearded blond man with shadows under his eyes. He was wearing a black uniform instead of a white coat, and there wasn't a stethoscope around his neck, but something made her certain he was a doctor. She raised her head and grabbed his hand. "Where am I? Where's Piper? What happened!"

The moment her hand touched his, a brilliant blue spark arced between them, bright enough to dazzle her eyes. *No.* She snatched her hand back as disbelief and denial hit her like a one-two punch. "Please tell me you're human and that was just a bit of static discharge."

He stared at her for a long moment before answering. "I am Pyrosian, not human. You're aboard one of our ships, the *Firebrand*. You were badly injured in the attack…" He raised his hand, his gaze locked on the point where the blue spark had struck his skin. "This can't be."

Haley was trying to sort through too much information to make sense of any of it. "I'm on a ship? In space? No, no, no. You're not supposed to take women who weren't matched!" She'd read the rules, and they were very clear about that. Consent was important. She tried to sit up, but the moment she moved, the blond snapped out of his fugue and put a hand on her shoulder, gently pushing her back down.

"Lie still."

She glowered at him. "You don't get to tell me what to do."

He met her gaze, his green eyes narrowed and his square jaw set in a stubborn line. "When you arrived here, your skull was fractured in multiple places and you were bleeding internally. Until I am satisfied you are fully healed, you are in my care, and that means I do, in fact, get to tell you what to do. Now, lie down and stay still."

"Fractured? How long have I been here?" She reached up to touch the back of her head, expecting to find some evidence of what he was saying. Shaved hair. Wounds. At least a bandage. There was nothing out of place.

"You were found shortly after the attack and brought here for treatment. That was yesterday. You should recover rapidly, but it will still be a few days before you are back to full strength."

"I was with someone. A woman with blue hair and a double dose of attitude."

He shook his head, his expression regretful. "I'm sorry. I haven't seen anyone matching that description, and I've been here since the first patients arrived."

"But that was yesterday! How can you still be on your feet?"

"I was needed." The blond shrugged as if staying up for more than a day was nothing special. "You're the one who needs rest."

"I'll rest later. Right now, I want answers. Was that really the Spark? What's your name? How can I find out what happened to my friends?"

He ignored her questions. "You'll rest *now*." He pressed something on the panel above her head, and the world started to slip away again.

"Don't you dare—" she managed, before the darkness rose up and claimed her again.

* * *

TOREL STARED down at the unconscious female and swore under his breath. "Flames and fury. I'm mated."

He reached for his mate's hand, craving contact. As his fingers closed around hers, he tried to make it look as if he were merely checking her pulse rate. A weak ruse, considering her bio-readings were clearly displayed on the monitor above her head.

He withdrew his hand and fisted it at his side, determined not to touch her again until she regained consciousness. He'd only given her a light dose of sedative; she'd be awake again soon. He shouldn't have sedated her at all, but she was still recovering from her injuries, and he didn't want to jeopardize her health with any sudden shocks – like confirming the spark she'd seen wasn't static discharge, but destiny.

All he knew about the female the Gods had sent to disrupt his life was that she was tall for a human female, with a thick mane of red-brown hair and dark eyes. Her voice had been pleasing, and her questions had been intelligent and succinct. The monitor's data showed she was in her mid-thirties by human measurements, and she was in good health apart from her recent injuries. It wasn't enough. "I don't even know your name," he murmured softly.

He wanted to know more. Flames. He wanted to know everything, and they'd barely met. How was he going to help save his race if he couldn't focus on anything but her?

"Torel? We're having trouble stabilizing one of the human patients." One of his staff interrupted his musings.

"Which one?"

"Keth's mate, Eva."

He should have guessed. She'd undergone two bouts of extensive treatment, but something wasn't right. The scans didn't show anything, but there was too much they didn't know about human biology. "I'll be right there. How is Keth coping?"

The medic gave a quick shake of his head. "If she doesn't wake soon, he'll have to be placed in stasis."

It wasn't ideal, but it was the only option they had. Once the Scorching had started, there was no way to stop it. With Eva too injured to consummate the mating, Keth had no way to ease the mating fever. "Better get him prepped. He doesn't have much time."

He looked down at the sleeping female. Because of her, he was running out of time, too. No one in the thrall of the Scorching was allowed to remain on duty. He needed to inform his second in command and step down as the chief medical officer until he was clearheaded again. Those were the rules. He'd enforced them himself, more than once. He thought he'd understood the sense of powerlessness and frustration Commander Denza and the others had felt. He hadn't then, but he did now.

He had a little time left. He'd use it to do what he could for Keth and his mate. Maybe by then, he'd have some idea what to say to his own mate.

He should probably start by introducing himself.

WHEN TOREL finally informed his staff what had happened, they were uniformly delighted. Their enthusiasm far exceeded his own and they shooed him out of the medical center with instructions to shower and change before his mate saw him again. He'd been officially relieved of duty and a team would transfer his mate to his rooms. Until the Scorching ended, she would be his only patient.

By the time he stepped out of the shower, a hushed murmur of voices came from the main room of his quarters. He dressed quickly, donning a comfortable pair of pants and a dark, sleeveless shirt. The Scorching was already starting to affect him strongly, wreaking havoc with both his body and his mind. His skin was sensitive, and his cock was in a perpetual state of arousal. The thought of wearing anything heavy or fitted was decidedly unappealing.

Worse than the physical changes were the mental ones. It was hard to focus on even the simplest task, and he grew more and more agitated the longer he was separated from his mate.

"Why have you done this to me?" he muttered. Not that he expected an answer. The Gods didn't have to explain their decisions. It was up to their followers to accept what came and find a way to make it work somehow. There was always a way. With that thought fixed in his mind, he squared his shoulders and re-entered the main room.

He padded barefoot across the room to the edge of his bed and looked down at his mate. She was still sleeping, but her hands moved restlessly across the covers. Her cheeks were flushed, too, and a quick touch to her brow confirmed that her temperature was slightly elevated. The Scorching had taken hold of her as well.

"She's rousing quickly, sir," one of the medical staff informed him as they prepared to depart.

"I can see that. What were her scans like before you moved her?"

"Her fractures are ninety-four percent set and healing well. Only small traces of soft tissue damage remaining. No cognitive or neurological issues detected. She's been cleared for full release into your care. If she needs pain medication, a droid will bring it to you."

"Thank you."

They left, but he barely registered their departure. All his attention was on her. The need to touch her was a physical ache, but he resisted. Instead, he sat on the edge of the bed, close enough he could feel the heat of her body soaking into his skin even through the light sheet they had tucked in around her. She was garbed in the standard pale-yellow pajamas issued to all patients, and his mind was full of images what she'd look like once he'd torn them off her.

He fisted his hands on his thighs and exhaled sharply. That was not going to happen. Even if it killed him.

HALEY WOKE up much faster this time. The moment she was fully awake, she knew something was different. The lighting, the feel of the bed, the sounds, even the scent of the air had changed. She opened her eyes and sat up, determined not to let anyone push her around this time.

One thing was the same. The blond guy beside her, only this time he was sitting on a bed. An actual bed. She whipped her head around, ignoring the dizzy spell the motion caused. Bed. Furniture. Soft colours. Carpets. This was not the same place she had woken up last time. "Where am I? Who the hell are you? And before you answer, don't think I don't remember you were the one who roofied me when I asked too many questions. Do that again and I'll...I'll write something scathing about you and your people and make sure the government hears what you did."

He gave her a lopsided grin that made him look sexy as hell. Her anger vanished, seared away by a sudden, powerful rush of longing. She wanted him. Badly.

What the hell is going on?

"I will answer your questions in order. You are in my quarters. I know that seems strange, but I will explain the reasons soon. My name is Torel Zinn, and I am the Chief Medical Officer assigned to the *Firebrand,* the royal flagship of the Pyrosian fleet. As for my choice to sedate you, I am sorry about that. I was worried the shock of what had just happened would be detrimental to your recovery."

She stared at him and tried to recall the details of their first meeting. What had happened that would shock her? She woke up, asked about Piper and then —"Oh shit, the Spark."

"The Spark," he repeated, nodding. "Do you know what it represents?"

"Your people believe it means we're a good match, right? That's what the Gathering was supposed to be about. Getting potential matches together to see if they initiate a spark." He hesitated just long enough for her reporter instincts to buzz. "What am I missing?" she asked.

"The Spark is more than an indication of compatibility. It indicates that we have found our true mate. It also heralds the onset of what we call the Scorching."

"And what the hell is that? The information you people sent out didn't mention anything about this Scorching thing." She leaned forward, ignoring the fact the move put them even closer together. She could smell the soap he'd used, a subtle musky scent that made her want to bury her nose in the crook of his neck and breathe deep.

What the fuck is wrong with me?

She forced herself to focus. "I'm a journalist, and I'm seriously considering writing an exposé on all of this. First, my friend hits the wrong button and ends up matched with no way to opt out, and now you're telling me we're matched even though I never even signed up! This smells like a scam."

His brows furrowed, and the corners of his mouth turned downward. "It is not a scam. And this was not something I intended to happen. This was the Gods' doing, not mine. I have patients I should be attending to right now, but instead I have to be here, with you."

She huffed in frustration. "No, you don't. You can go back to work any time you want. Just leave me some clothes and tell me how to get back to Earth so I can look for my friends."

"You don't understand. I must be here." He took her hand and held it. "You are my mate, and we are both experiencing the Scorching, the mating fever. I'm sorry. I wish things could be different. Flames, I don't even know your name."

"Woah." She tugged her hand out of his grip and scrambled toward the middle of the bed. "Mating fever? Is that why I'm in your bedroom instead of the medical center? Oh, hell no. Give me one good reason I shouldn't start screaming for help right now."

"Well, for one thing, this room is relatively soundproof. For another, we're in orbit around your planet. Just how far do you think you can shout?" He was grinning as he said it, and there was nothing but laughter in his pale green eyes.

"It's not funny!" She snapped.

His smile vanished. "You're right, it's not. I'm sorry, *otama*. This is all very strange for me, too. I shouldn't have laughed or teased you." He reached his hand out to her again, but this time he held it steady a foot away from her. "I promise you, nothing will happen between us without your consent."

"Swear to your Gods?"

All trace of levity left his expression, and his next

words were spoken with utter sincerity. "I swear by the Flames of the First Ones that nothing will happen between us without your express consent. Furthermore, at the end of the Scorching, you will be free to return to Earth if you choose."

"Thank you. My name's Haley, by the way. Haley Anderson." She took his hand expecting him to shake it. Instead, he raised it to his lips and feathered a barely-there kiss across her knuckles.

"It is an honour to meet you, Haley Anderson."

"Hang on, I didn't agree to that!"

He gave her a puzzled look, his head cocked to one side. "That is how males greet females of your species, is it not? I watched several entertainment productions indicating this."

"You watched movies? That is how you learned about human women?" Laughter bubbled up inside her and before she could stop herself, she was giggling. Giggles turned to guffaws, and by the time she regained her composure, her ribs ached. She felt a little better though, as if her short lapse had helped her get a grip.

"Princess Maggie and her ladies made me watch some of their favourites on the journey here. They believed it would help us with the newly matched females. Was this wrong?"

She almost started giggling all over again. "No, not wrong. But, there's a bit more to understanding a woman than just watching a few movies."

"I know. The males who were matched were given more detailed instruction and extensive cognitive augmentation. Language. Slang. Customs and traditions. I wasn't matched, though. You were a surprise." He smiled a little, and her heart fluttered as a dimple appeared in his cheek. This situation would be easier to navigate if he wasn't so damned hot.

"So, what happens now, Torel?" she used his name for the first time.

He interwove their fingers and set his hand down on top of one hard thigh. "Do you wish me to explain it in medical terms, or simplify it for now?"

"Let's start simple. Give me an overview, and then I'll know what questions I want to ask." The way she was feeling right now, simple was better. Her train of thought kept being derailed by X-rated thoughts of the handsome man holding her hand.

"As you wish." His thumb drew slow circles over the back of her hand as he spoke. "The Scorching is our word for the mating fever that comes after the Spark. It lasts approximately two of your days and is a time of intense sexual desire and intimacy. When it is over, we will be permanently connected by a psychic link. The strength varies, but at a minimum, we will be able to sense each other's presence."

She blew out a slow breath. "Ookaay. You're telling me I'm going to want to get naked and wild with you for the next two days. That's not so bad. You're attractive, but I think I can resist you for forty-eight hours. Problem solved."

"It is not that simple. One of the reasons I sedated you is to slow the onset of your symptoms. Soon you'll be feeling what I am." He touched his chest. "My skin is sensitive to the slightest touch. My pulse is elevated, my body temperature is rising, and it is becoming increasingly difficult to resist the urge to touch you. As time passes, my primal instincts will overpower everything else, and so will yours."

"So, you're saying resistance is futile? Dear god, I've landed in the middle of someone's Star Trek fanfic, haven't I?"

"Resistance would be futile. The longer we resist, the more discomfort we will experience, but it won't change the outcome. And before you ask, there is no way to reverse this or prevent it from happening."

"I thought you said nothing would happen without my consent? The way you're describing it, my options are to agree to have sex with you now, or suffer a great deal of discomfort and end up having sex with you anyway. That's not much of a choice."

Torel was quiet for a moment, his free hand stroking the short length of beard covering his jaw. "Your culture has something called a one-night stand, correct? Two people coming together for a brief period of pleasure, with no expectations. Would it be easier to think of this as a two-night stand?"

She started to bristle at the suggestion but stopped when she realized it *did* make it easier. She liked sex. In the years since Jeff's death, she'd been with other men. Hooking up was easy. It was the messy, emotional stuff she wanted to avoid. If Torel was being honest about what he wanted, then this might actually work. "Is that what you want? I thought mating was supposed to be a huge deal for you guys. Bound for life, never want another woman and all that?"

"We do mate for life, and once the bond is sealed, I will never desire any other female." He tightened his grip on her fingers and gazed into her eyes. "But I never wanted to be mated. I have dedicated my life to helping my race restore our population, and by extension, I am learning all I can about human females and the children they will produce with their Pyrosian mates. That is my priority. It has to be."

She reached up and touched his face, running her fingertips gently from temple to chin. He was handsome, confident, and willing to be open with her about how he felt. "You're suggesting that when this Scorching thing is over, we go our separate ways? You head home, and I go back to Earth?"

He turned and brushed a kiss to her fingers, then started to nibble at her fingertips. "I think we can make that work, yes. If you are agreeable, we can meet up whenever my people come to your planet to gather more matched females."

She laughed. "So, I'd be your intergalactic booty call?"

"If that phrase means what I think it does, then yes. You will be my booty call. Is this acceptable to you?" His last words were pitched low and came out with a primal growl that made her toes tingle.

"Growl like that again, and I'll agree to anything

you want." The words were past her lips before the thought had fully formed in her mind.

Any other man would have reacted with a joke or a cocky comment. Torel didn't. His eyes blazed a brilliant gold, and a low growl rumbled up from deep in his chest as he closed the short distance between them and crushed his mouth to hers. For one brief second she resisted him. But then the flames of her desire grew into an inferno, burning away every doubt and argument. She wanted him. He wanted her. They'd figure out everything else later. Much later.

CHAPTER THREE

For the first time in his adult life, Torel wasn't in complete control. He'd lost the battle the moment Haley spoke. A tiny voice in the back of his mind insisted what she said wasn't a proper invitation to kiss her, but it was drowned out by a triumphant roar that repeated a single word. "Mine."

All his discipline, restraint, and focus were reduced to ash as the Scorching ignited in a firestorm of wants and needs. He gathered Haley into his arms and held her, needing to feel the press of her body against him. She came to him willingly, wrapping her arms around his neck and responding to his kisses with sultry moans that made his dick hard enough to pierce hull plating. He wanted to tear her clothes off and spread her out on the bed like a feast, but he refused to give in completely. She was still recovering from her injuries, and he would not do anything to risk her health. *Slow. I have to go slow,* he reminded himself, but it was a battle he couldn't win. He might as well have tried to change the trajectory of a comet with his bare hands.

His tongue tangled with hers as they ground their bodies together. Her nails scraped the back of his neck with enough force to sting, and the sweet bite of pain blended with the pleasure of having her in his arms.

She tore her mouth from his to stare at him, cheeks flushed, lips swollen from his kisses, and her eyes bright with desire. "Two days of this?" she asked.

"Yes. And this is only the beginning, *otama*." Until the Scorching ended, they would be driven to mate over and over, with only brief periods of respite to eat and sleep.

Her mouth quirked up into a dazzling smile that sent all the blood in his body straight to his cock. "I really think you guys should mention this bit in the brochure. You'd probably be overwhelmed with women wanting to sign up."

"But how many of them would want to travel to a new planet and leave everyone they know behind?" He didn't want a permanent mating, but he was a special case. Every other male he knew dreamed of the day they'd find their match and claim their mate forever.

"Right. That's an issue. It's one of the reasons my friend was going to turn down her match." She paled. "Oh my god, I forgot about Aria. And Piper! How could I forget about my friends like that? I don't even know if they survived. What kind of friend am I?"

"There were no fatalities among the human females,

so your friends must be alright." He started to undress her as he spoke, the need to get her naked at war with his desire to comfort her. "As for what kind of friend you are? One of the first things you asked me as you woke up was if I knew what had happened to your blue-haired companion. You are not a poor friend, you are in the thrall of the Scorching. It is very difficult to think about anyone or anything else during this time." He gave up trying to unhook the simple fastening of her top and tore it open.

She glanced down at her torn outfit and chuckled. "Feeling a bit of the thrall yourself?"

"Yes." He reached for her again, barely managing to stop himself before making contact. "Do I have your permission?"

She looked down at his hands, then back to his face. "This isn't going to stop until we do this, right?"

"I'm afraid not." He didn't tell her that if they didn't complete their mating, there was a good chance he'd be either insane or dead in a matter of days. She might only have the barest illusion of choice, but he wasn't going to take that from her by telling her the whole truth.

To his relief and delight, she shrugged out of the torn remnants of her top, baring her body to him. "Then yes, you have my permission." She flashed him a wicked little grin. "Do I have yours?"

"Flames and fury, yes, you do." He closed in for a kiss, drinking her in as he gathered her into his arms and let his weight carry them both down to the mattress. His hands roamed over her body and his tongue danced with hers. The air around them nearly sizzled with heat as they came together, hands stroking skin and tugging at clothing. He breathed in, and the scent of her arousal filled his lungs.

Her fingers stroked the bare skin of his back, and he belatedly realized he'd removed his shirt. He didn't remember doing it, but that was immaterial. All that mattered was that her hands were on his body, and nothing had ever felt so good.

He slid a hand between them, cupping one pert breast against his palm. She moaned and arched herself against his hand. His touch grew rougher and more demanding as his control slipped another notch. Her eager reactions inflamed him further, every moan and wriggle tearing away another layer of control. Cloth tore, pillows were flung aside in their quest to get naked without letting go of one other.

Flames, she is glorious. The thought took him by surprise. He'd never given much thought to having a mate, but now she was here, she took his breath away.

"What did you say?" Her words were barely more than a whisper against his lips.

He hadn't realized he'd spoken aloud. "I said you were glorious. That is the correct word, isn't it?"

She beamed up at him. "I like it."

Her words pleased him more than they should. Feeling off-balance, he kissed her again, moving from her lips to her jaw, then down to the pulse point just below her ear. He brushed away the thick locks of her hair, exposing her throat. Inch by inch he savoured her, working slowly down her body until his mouth found one diamond-hard nipple. He sucked and nibbled at it, enjoying her soft cries of pleasure.

"More," she whispered, her fingers sliding into his hair to pull him closer.

A dark, dangerous thought crept into his consciousness, and he gave into it, closing his teeth around her delicate bud with just enough force to sting. She shuddered beneath him, her fingers tightening their grip as she voiced a wild, keening cry of pure need.

He released her, lifting his head to stare into her eyes. "I don't want to hurt—"

She tugged at his hair and shook her head. "You won't. Stop thinking so much, Tor."

"That's not my name."

"And mine's not *otama*."

He growled in frustration and she grinned. "That's better."

He bowed his head, claiming the other nipple and giving it the same treatment as the first. Each time his teeth grazed the diamond-hard nub she responded with such passion it made his cock ache. She was caught up completely in the Scorching, now, and he loved her this way, wild, wanton, and eager.

All the hours he'd spent studying human anatomy came into use in new ways as he used his knowledge to seek out every sensitive spot he could reach while still worshipping her breasts, laving first one and then the other. Soon, he was so aroused his hands shook as he caressed her.

She parted her thighs, wordlessly inviting him to continue his carnal exploration. He gave her nipple one last nip before settling between her legs. She reached for her pussy and he caught her hand at the wrist, stopping her. "Hands at your sides. The only one who gets to touch you right now is me."

Her brown eyes widened, and for a second he thought she was going to protest, but when he let go of her she followed his directions. It was flaming sexy the way she obeyed him, especially since he didn't think she was normally submissive. "I'm being good. I think I should get a reward for that."

He chuckled. "I think so, too." He stroked his hands up the soft flesh of her inner thighs, moving upward until his fingers reached the slick lips of her pussy. Her breath hitched when he pushed a finger into her folds and stroked the swollen pearl of her clitoris. Her next breath came out in a needy moan, and he gave in to the white-hot need to taste her. He spread her legs wider and lowered himself between them, so his mouth was tantalizingly close to her pussy.

Using his thumbs to part her labia, he moved so close his breath fanned over her slick flesh. "Is this what you want?"

"Do you really have to ask?" she retorted, her words tinged with sexual frustration.

Her sassy response made him laugh as he bowed his head and gave her the reward they both craved.

THE SECOND HIS tongue touched her clit, Haley was lost. Every word and thought in her head vaporized in an instant, leaving her with nothing to focus on but the pleasure Torel gave her. His beard rasped against her tender flesh while his tongue and fingers worked her clit without mercy. When his fingers slid into her channel she gasped and then cried out his name as he expertly curved his hand to stroke over the hidden spot that maximized her pleasure.

She rode his fingers, rubbing her pussy against his talented tongue. Soon, she was gripping the bedsheets, her clit throbbing in time to her hammering heartbeat. His every touch pushed her closer to the brink, and still he drove her onward until her senses were reeling, and she teetered on the edge of ecstasy. Drunk on pleasure, she became a creature of pure sensation, soaring higher than she'd ever believed possible. When she came, it was so intense she felt like she was falling, only to be caught in Torel's arms as she slowly came back to her senses.

It took all her strength to lift her head to look at him as he rose to his knees and wiped his mouth with the back of one hand. His blond hair was tousled, his expression smug, and his eyes shimmered with what she swore was a golden hue.

"Your eyes keep changing colours," she said, raising a shaking hand to point to his face.

"To gold?"

She nodded. "That's supposed to happen?"

"It is. Once we are mated, my eyes will stay gold for the rest of my life. It's a symbol of my status as a mated male."

"You're going to have to explain all this to me later. But for now," she opened her arms and smiled at him. "I think it's time we finished what you started."

"Flames and fury, I think so, too."

Every part of her hummed with anticipation as he moved over her, his gaze never leaving hers. She liked the way he looked at her as if she were the only thing that mattered to him. It had been a long time since anyone had looked at her that way.

She slammed the brakes on that line of thinking. Now was no time to remember the past, and whatever this Scorching was, it wasn't going to last. A few days of hot sex and laughter, and then they would both go back to their regular lives.

He kissed her passionately, his lean, hard body settling into the cradle of her thighs and his cock nestled right against her entrance. She kissed him back, setting her hands on his powerful shoulders. She opened herself to him, one leg bent with her foot flat against the mattress.

They came together, the thick head of his cock sliding into her body at the perfect angle, sending a cascade of sensation sweeping through her.

He murmured something in another language, and once again his eyes flashed a brilliant gold.

"What was that?"

"We are one," he whispered before kissing her with so much heat she wondered if the sheets were fireproof.

"Yes, we are, and it feels amazing." She wriggled her hips. "Show me more, spaceman."

He growled and thrust deeper, then withdrew and did it again. He was bigger than most of her other lovers, stretching her body in delightful ways. She rose up to meet his next thrust, moaning into his mouth as pleasure and pain blended into one breathtaking sensation. They'd barely begun, and she already knew the next two days would include some of the best sex of her life.

They raced each other up the scales of pleasure, both of them doing all they could to push the other to orgasm first. He groaned as she closed her teeth on his lower lip, and she gasped every time he shifted the angle of their bodies to ensure her clit was being caressed with every thrust. She tore her mouth from his to bury her head in the crook of his neck, breathing in his scent as she raked his back with her nails.

He shuddered and groaned her name, his strokes growing more urgent, his pace more unsteady. He pushed himself upward, his arms flexing as he opened space between their bodies. "Touch yourself, now," he demanded.

She reached between her legs, working her clit between her fingers as he continued to fuck her with wild, eager thrusts. Soon, she was quaking, on the cusp of release.

He roared her name as he drove into her one last

time. He erupted inside of her, his cock thickening until the pressure sent her spiralling into yet another orgasm. If the rest of their time together was this good, she'd happily pencil Torel in for more intergalactic hookups every time he came to Earth.

CHAPTER FOUR

THEY STAYED TOGETHER in a tangle of limbs for a long time, and when he finally eased himself off her, it was only to flop down beside her with a contented grunt.

"I second that," she murmured, nestling into his side. It was another minute before she had the strength to open her eyes and look at him. His eyes were the colour of molten gold, now. "Your eyes look incredible."

"As do yours." He stroked his thumb over her cheek. "Do you wish to see for yourself?"

"Wait, what?" Adrenaline surged, erasing her post-coital fugue in an instant. "What about my eyes?"

"Humans mated to Pyrosians often have their eyes change colour, too. That information was to be revealed when Princess Maggie, Lisa, and Gwen arrived at the Gathering."

"But I've seen pictures of the princess and the woman spokeswoman for the agency, their eyes weren't gold."

"Pictures can be altered, and contact lens were used to conceal the truth during live interviews."

"You people sure have a lot of damned secrets." She looked around the room for a mirror. "I want to see my eyes. What do they look like?"

He spoke some kind of command in his own language and a few seconds later the wall behind the bed turned into a mirror. She stared at her reflection in disbelief. "My eyes are gold?"

"They are." Torel moved in behind her, looking into the mirror as well. "You look even more lovely this way."

"But. Gold." She waved at her reflection. "That's going to be a little hard to explain to my parents. They already don't approve of my life choices, and this little plot-twist isn't going to help. Hey Mom and Dad, I banged a hot alien and these were a side effect. Surprise!"

He stared at her through the mirror, his expression suddenly stormy. "Why wouldn't your parents approve of your choices? You are an intelligent, well-spoken, and attractive female. What choice did you make that they didn't approve of?"

"If we're going to talk about my parents, I'm going to need booze."

"Booze?" he queried.

"Uh, liquor? Any kind of alcoholic beverage. Surely your species has that."

"Ah, I see. Yes, we have alcoholic drinks. But, you really shouldn't consume any, yet."

"Why not?" The answer dawned on her a split-second later. "This is about my head injury, right?"

"It is. The medications you've been given would be impeded if you drank alcohol. You are not one hundred percent healed and won't be for another day or so."

"I find your diagnosis a little suspect. If I'm not healed enough to enjoy a drink, how can I be well enough to be doing the horizontal tango with you?"

This time, he caught her meaning without help. "If we hadn't mated, we would both be suffering right now. It was a calculated risk, one I didn't take lightly. If any of my colleagues had disagreed, I would have placed myself in stasis and waited for you to recover. That situation is currently playing out with another male who found his mate in the aftermath of the bombing. She was badly injured, and her recovery has been complicated. Keth had to be placed in stasis for his own protection."

"Protect him from what, exactly? You said it would get very unpleasant for both of us if we didn't mate." She turned from the mirror to look at him directly. "You didn't tell me everything, did you?"

He wrapped her in his arms and kissed her gently before answering. "If you had refused to mate with me, there were only two outcomes for me. Insanity, or death."

"You should have told me!" She cradled his face in her hands, trying to understand why he hadn't said anything.

"If I'd told you, would you have considered saying no?" he asked.

"Of course not!"

"And that is why I didn't say anything. It had to be your choice."

She stared at him, dumbfounded. "You're crazy. It's just sex, right?"

"It still had to be your decision. I saw what happened the last time we came to Earth. The females did not react well to their lack of choices. In the end, all of them chose to stay with their mates, but it was not an easy transition. Our situation is different, because, as you say, it's a temporary sexual relationship, but I still wanted you to have a choice."

"What would have happened to me if I'd said no?"

Torel was quiet for a long moment. "That is a question I can't answer. You only have a small amount of Pyrosian genes, but it was enough to initiate the Scorching and change your eye colour. I didn't consider the risk to you." He bowed his head. "Forgive me."

She nudged his chin back up so she could look into his eyes. "There's nothing to forgive. This Scorching thing packs a serious punch. Neither of us has been thinking clearly." Considering she'd just had sex with an alien from another planet, that might be the understatement of the year.

"This clarity of mind will not last long, either. Before it fades, I want to know why your parents aren't proud of you."

"If I can't have a drink, how about something to eat? We can have a bed picnic while I tell you about my parents, and you can tell me something about yourself, too. We're going to be together for two more days. I'd like to know more than just your name."

"Food is a good idea." He raised his head higher and spoke in his own language again, then lowered his voice and explained. "I just requested the computer send a service droid with a selection of food choices approved for human consumption."

"How do you know which stuff to approve?" Once the Scorching was over, Haley was going to sit down with Torel and anyone else she could find and start asking questions. Lots of questions. She was already envisioning a running series of stories about the Pyrosians and their quest for mates. There was so much to tell. It wouldn't be an attack piece, but something informative, and hopefully interesting. This was going to be how she was going to prove herself to her father.

"I'll tell you if you lie back down and rest while we wait for our meal."

"Is this your subtle way of trying to tell me what to do again?"

"I wasn't trying to be subtle. You need to rest while you can," he said, gesturing to the bed.

"Bossy Torel is not my favourite. He's not even in the top two," she declared, but she settled back on the bed. The truth was, she did feel a little tired. Not that she was going to admit it.

"You don't have to like him, but I hope you'll listen to him anyway." His tone softened as she did as he asked. "What are your top two, then? Or is that who? My language lessons didn't include speaking about different parts of my own personality."

"Oh, that's easy. Growly Torel is my favourite, followed by the version of you that actually makes jokes and laughs. I'm not a fan of super serious Torel, either."

He stretched out beside her on the bed and covered them both with a portion of the blankets. "I don't think you'll be seeing too much of him. For the next two cycles, I have been stripped of all duties but one – taking care of you."

"Stripped of duty?" She didn't like the way that sounded. "Why?"

"It's a rule. No one experiencing the Scorching can be on active duty unless circumstances are dire. I can't care for my patients properly if I'm only thinking about you."

She nodded. "Makes sense. I wish some of the doctors on Earth had a similar rule. If Jeff's doctor hadn't been going through a nasty divorce, maybe he would have caught the cancer early enough to save him."

"Jeff?"

Shit. Why did I bring him up? "Jeff was my husband. He died of cancer a few years ago."

Torel hugged her but released her quickly when she

didn't return the hug. "I'm sorry. That must have been a very difficult time for you."

"Thank you. It was awful, but I got through it with the help of a dear friend." She had learned to dread people's reaction when she told them she was a widow. They never seemed to know what to say. They might babble, or they'd stop talking altogether. The worst were the ones who told her she'd find someone new or that everything happened for a reason. She'd lost someone she loved, watched him suffer and fight for months, and in the end, the grief had nearly killed her. If there was a reason for that, then she wanted to know what the hell it was.

"Your friend, was she the one with you yesterday?"

"One of them, yeah. Aria was here to meet her match. Not that she wanted to be matched. It was an accident. By the way, you guys really need to put an undo button on your app. If you had one, she would have been able to back out gracefully. Not that I think she should have. I mean, what if the guy really was her perfect mate? What if he was okay with her having a baby already?"

Torel's golden eyes widened. "Your friend has a child? That…we never considered that scenario."

"She's got an adorable ten-month-old daughter, which she thinks will be more than enough of a reason for her match to reject her."

He shook his head. "On the contrary, I suspect most males offered a chance to have not only a mate but also a daughter to care for would be ecstatic."

"Really? You guys are that keen on kids?" She frowned. "Are *you*? Keen to have kids, I mean."

He looked at her in bemusement. "Until a few hours ago, I had not considered even having a mate. Offspring were not something I'd contemplated at all."

"That's not an answer." Before she could press him for a more decisive one, there was an electronic three-note warble. "What was that?"

"Our meal is arriving." Torel pointed to the wall beside the door. Part of it vanished, and something that looked like a cross between R2D2 and a room service cart wheeled in through the gap. It was laden with covered dishes, bowls of fresh fruit, and several pitchers, some covered in condensation, indicating the contents were chilled.

"Can I get one of those to take home with me? I seem to live on takeout these days."

"You should take better care of yourself than that. Though I confess, I would probably be in the same situation as you if I didn't have service droids to purchase, prepare, and serve my meals on schedule. I often get so caught up in my work I forget to eat."

"Sign me up for service droids. Maybe you can bring me one the next time you visit."

"I'll see what I can do."

"You know, I'm not the only woman on the planet who doesn't want the whole committed relationship thing. Maybe you should consider bringing some of your unmatched males to Earth next time you visit. There aren't enough women on your planet, right? So, they can't be getting much uh…quality time with a woman until they're mated. They could even stay on Earth to act like sexy goodwill ambassadors."

She'd been joking, mostly, but Torel didn't crack the barest hint of a smile.

"Come on, that was at least a little bit funny, wasn't it?" Had she hit a taboo subject or something?

Torel rose from the bed to fetch their meals without responding to Haley's comments. The idea of having ambassadors on Earth was intriguing, but unlikely to come to anything given the way the Gathering had been attacked. Coming to acquire more matched females and conduct trade was one thing, but allowing males to remain on the planet alone would be a serious risk to take. It wasn't until he turned back with the first tray of food that he realized she was looking at him expectantly. "I'm sorry. I started thinking about your suggestion and failed to reply."

"Yeah, you did. I was starting to wonder if I'd upset you somehow." She took the tray from him and started re-arranging the blankets to make a makeshift platform for their food.

"Not at all. It was an interesting idea." He continued talking while going back for another tray. "The sexual ambassador aspect wouldn't work, though. Unlike you, we can only reach sexual release with our destined mates."

Behind him, Haley made an alarming choking noise that had him at her side in seconds.

"What is it? Are you in pain?"

She gave him a wild-eyed look and sputtered again. "Only with your mate? Holy shit, Tor. You've never gotten off before? *Ever*?"

It took him a moment to work out her meaning. "Not until just now, with you."

"I'm starting to think your Gods have a mean streak. What happened in the days before you had genetic testing and databases? How many of your people went their whole lives never finding a mate or even getting to enjoy sex?" she demanded.

"Not as many as you'd think. In those times, Gatherings were held often, and those who had yet to find their mates would attend as many as possible, often travelling long distances. It's an imperfect system, but so are the courtship rituals of your world."

"Well, you're not wrong about that, but at least we can still have orgasms. I still think your Gods are assholes."

He chuckled. The Gods had dragged both of them into this mating without consideration for their feelings or plans. "You're not wrong about that, either, though my mother would scold me if she heard me say so."

"I bet she wouldn't. You're everything a mother could want in a son. Handsome. Successful. Clearly affluent enough to have your own fleet of service droids taking care of you. I bet she'd forgive you just about anything."

He finished bringing over the food and dishes and then wheeled the droid close to the bed so they could reach the pitchers of liquid. Serving others wasn't something he did, but there was something about Haley—He pushed the thought aside. It had to be the Scorching. That was all. These feelings would fade once the mating fever ended. Mates travelled separately all the time. This wouldn't be any different.

He reclaimed his place at Haley's side and started uncovering dishes. There was a wide variety, including some of his favourites, both entrees and desserts. "My mother thinks I work too hard and do not give the Gods enough credit, and while she is proud of me, she has made it clear I'm the one she worries about the most. Apparently, she wants more from me than a life of duty and research."

"Like a mate?" Haley asked around a mouthful of thickly iced brownie.

It was one of the desserts Gwen, Kash's human mate, had taught the palace kitchen staff to prepare. He hadn't been surprised to see it had made to the menu of the *Firebrand*. "I don't think she's concerned about the specifics. She just wants me to enjoy life more. I think that's what most parents want for their younglings, isn't it?"

"Not my parents. They think they know exactly what I should be doing, and with who. My mother gave me exactly three months to mourn for Jeff, and then she started pressuring me to find someone new. Preferably one of the men she had selected for me. Wealthy, elite, corporate types, for the most part. All card-carrying members of her social circle, of course. She never approved of Jeff, and she is determined not to let me make the same *mistake* again."

She did her best to hide it, but he could hear the pain behind her words. "She called your choice in mates a mistake? Why? Weren't you happy?"

"I was very happy...and very broke. Jeff was an environmentalist. I met him when I was doing a story about the activists trying to block a major oil pipeline. He was arrested the first time we met. He had so much passion for his cause, and for life in general. He was like no one I'd ever met before. My parents were horrified, and I didn't care. In fact, it made him even more attractive to me."

He wanted to hear more, but it also bothered him a little to see her so animated about another male, even one who was no longer among the living. "So he was from a different class than you and your parents. I thought such issues were no longer important to humans, at least, not the ones from your geographic location."

"Oh, it still matters to some people. Especially the ones who come from old money like my parents. My mother never worked a day in her life, and my father inherited the family business, a newspaper. The only reason Mom got over the idea of me working at all was because I was their only child, and Dad wanted me to learn the trade so I could take over someday. The day I told them I was engaged to Jeff, Dad gave me an ultimatum. Leave Jeff or leave the newspaper."

Stunned to silence, Torel set aside his meal and moved in closer to Haley, nearly upsetting several of the dishes on the way. He set his hand on her shoulder and squeezed gently. "You deserve to be happy. Why wouldn't they want that for you?"

She looked up at him, and for one brief second, he saw a flash of hurt and confusion but as quickly as it came, it was gone again, replaced by a sardonic smile. "You'd have to ask them. Jeff's gone, I work for my father again, and they still haven't forgiven me for my little rebellion."

"You went back to work for your father after what he said? Why? Perhaps you should come to Pyros. No one would try to curtail your choices there." The words slipped out before he could stop them.

She stiffened, and her next words came out clipped and terse. "I went back because there wasn't any point in fighting with them any longer. Jeff was gone, and our plans died when he did."

"As for going to Pyros, what the hell would I do there? I don't even know your language. It's hard to be a journalist if you can't write in a language anyone can read. Besides, neither of us wants the messy reality of a mate, remember?"

"I remember." Torel wasn't even sure why he was discussing this. They had an arrangement already. She would stay on Earth and live her life, he would return to Pyros and his work. Simple. Uncomplicated. If she were on Pyros, things wouldn't stay simple.

"And how would it be on your world? Do mated couples often live separately there? I bet they don't. I wouldn't be escaping my problems, I'd just be exchanging them for different ones."

"I don't like the idea of you being unhappy, *otama*. We may be mated in name only, but the bond will still be there. I will know when your parents cause you upset."

"But you'll be halfway across the galaxy, how can you be sure the link will even stretch that far?"

"Your eyes turned gold. That's an indication your Pyrosian genes are no longer dormant." Yet another reason they were going to need some distance between them, it should weaken the effect of their bond.

"So, not everyone's eyes do this?" she asked.

"No. In fact, there's only been one other human whose eyes have turned gold..." He stopped as he realized there was something he'd forgotten to mention.

"What. What happened to the other woman?"

"Her name is Gwen, and she's fine. It's just that I failed to mention another possible outcome of our mating." He got out of bed, took a few steps away from her, and extended his hand. "I'm not actually sure how to—" A flame appeared in the middle of his palm. "Well, that was easier than I expected."

"What the flaming fuck are you doing?" Haley demanded, staring at his hand.

"My ability to manipulate fire has been unlocked by

our mating. It will take some time for me to be able to control it fully, but it shouldn't be an issue. As a precaution, all the furnishings and linens on this ship were made from fireproof materials."

"Hello. What about me? I'm not fireproof!"

"As my mate, you're immune to my fire." He snuffed out the flame and turned to face her. "As I am immune to yours."

"Mine? My what?"

"As I said, the only other mated human female I know with gold eyes is Gwen. She is also the only human female I know who can manipulate fire like a Pyrosian."

"Well, shit." She held her hand up. "I really hope this doesn't work."

He stayed silent as her brow furrowed and focused on her hand. Nothing happened. She shook her fingers and tried again, but no flame appeared. "Looks like you were wrong. No smoke. No fire."

"It might be too soon. You could try again in—" She cut him off.

"Nope. It's not happening. I have exceeded my capacity for weirdness for the year already. No Firestarter roles for me."

"That's not how it works." As much as he hoped she never manifested that ability, or anything else that indicated their bond was too strong to ignore, he knew her logic wasn't sound.

She fixed him with a determined stare. "Yes, it is. And even if it isn't, humour me and pretend. I just want to eat, talk, and hopefully get a little sleep before the Scorching makes us both lose our minds again."

He smiled and sat back down on the bed. She was clearly overwhelmed. Given how much she'd been hit with since waking up, she was coping amazingly well. He could humour her, for now. He pointed to one of the dishes. "I think you'll like this. It's Pyrosian, but many of the human females enjoy it. Apparently, it is very similar to something your people call a perogy."

She speared one of the dumplings and sampled it with obvious enjoyment. After that, they both did their best to keep the conversation light. By the time they had eaten their fill and set the dishes back on the service droid, Haley was yawning.

"It's time to rest, *otama*." He pulled back the covers and gestured for her to climb into bed.

"What's an *otama*, anyway?"

He settled in beside her and covered them both with the blankets. "It's a term of endearment that doesn't really translate into your language. I suppose it would be something close to sweetheart."

"If you're going to keep calling me that, I should have a nickname for you, too."

"You already do. You are the only person in the galaxy to ever call me Tor."

She snuggled into him with a contented sigh. "How long do you think we have before round two starts?"

"Long enough for us to get some rest." He draped an arm around her waist and pressed a kiss to the curve of her shoulder. "Sleep well."

"You, too."

As they both drifted off to sleep, Torel found himself wondering what it might be like to go to sleep every night with Haley in his arms. Not that it mattered. They weren't going to be together that often.

CHAPTER FIVE

HALEY WAS CURLED up in one of the two chairs placed in front of a floor to ceiling window in Torel's quarters. The chair molded to her form, cradling her comfortably, and there was a stunning view of Earth rotating just beneath them. She should be drinking it all in while she could, but she wasn't. There were more interesting things to look at. One was the breathtaking display of male beauty sitting across from her. Torel was comfortably sprawled in the other chair, completely naked. Neither of them had bothered getting dressed since they'd given in to the Scorching the day before. There wasn't much point when they never got more than an hour or two between rounds of mind-melting sex.

The other points of interest were currently scuttling around Torel's quarters, tidying up. She had discovered there were several different models of service droid, all with different functions. One droid was cleaning away the remains of their breakfast from the table between them, while another made up the bed with fresh linens. "I'm really starting to like having droids around to do all the work."

Torel glanced up from the tablet he'd been reading. "They do make life easier. I'm going to talk to Vadir about getting you one. It might take some time, though." He tapped the screen of the tablet. "I've been catching up on what's been happening, both here and on Earth. Some of the bombers have been captured, and the humans are working to identify others. Vadir and Prince Joran have been in almost constant contact with the many governments and leaders of your world, offering aid and trying to untangle this diplomatic mess."

"I think diplomacy takes precedence over my desire to have a robot to boss around, but thank you for thinking of me." In the short time they had been together, Torel had done that a lot. He'd anticipated her every want and need, in bed and out of it. Took note of the smallest details, down to what juice she preferred and how she took her coffee, then make sure that the next time, it was all just how she liked it. He'd arranged clothing to be delivered in her size, and while the fabrics and cut were a little different, she'd liked everything he'd selected.

Torel kept getting her to open up, too. She found herself chatting about everything from her work to her love of shoes, and in return he'd shared stories about his first trip to Earth, his parents and siblings, and the vacation he'd taken with them just before this mission. His affection for his family was obvious in the way he spoke of them, especially his mother.

He was finding ways past her defenses, and it worried her. She liked her life the way it was, safe and emotionally uncluttered. Aria was the one exception to that rule, and not even she knew everything about Haley's life.

"Obtaining a droid for you is a small matter. We may not be mates in the traditional sense, but I would still like to help you any way that I can." He shrugged, a gesture she had come to appreciate greatly. She loved the way his shoulder muscles flexed and moved when he did it.

"You don't need to give me presents or help me. I'm doing fine on my own," she replied.

"As you've already noted, I have the means. It would make me happy to be able to take care of you. I could find a droid with basic security functions. Your home is not the safest place, I'd like to know you were protected."

"My home is fine."

Torel set down the tablet on the table with a thump. "I was not referring to your domicile. I meant your city —your world. The attack the other day would never happen on Pyros. We have moved beyond that kind of fear-driven violence. Your people have not. I didn't understand how dangerous this world was. The attack did not kill any humans, but there were Pyrosian deaths. Young, hopeful males who came to Earth to claim their mates. This was supposed to help my people rebuild, not reduce our numbers further. This world is still very primitive in some ways. It's worrying."

She felt a stab of remorse. "I didn't know about the deaths. I'm sorry, Torel." She left her chair and circled around the small table to reach his side. He reached out a hand and she took it, letting him draw her into his lap.

"And I am sorry for my outburst. None of this is your fault. You were a victim, too. I just…" He smoothed her hair back from her face and kissed her brow. "I don't want anything to happen to you while I'm gone. We're connected, and that means I'll know if you are hurt with no way to get to you."

She still didn't really believe they'd be bonded that way. After all, she couldn't summon fire or do any of the other things the other mated human women could. She didn't have any powers or abilities. The only thing that had changed so far was her eyes. "I'll be fine. You'll be able to see for yourself the next time you come to visit. I live in a nice, safe building, I drive the speed limit, and the only thing I do to excess is drink wine with my friends." She stilled.

"Shit. Aria and Piper. While you were looking up the news, did you see anything about either of them?"

"I haven't checked recently." He twined one of her curls around his forefinger as he lifted his voice and began to speak in Pyrosian. The computer responded in the same language, and whatever it said must have been good news, because Torel started to smile.

"Well?" she demanded, impatient to know the details.

"Your friend Aria and her child are safe. In fact, she's on board the *Firebrand*."

She was so relieved she felt downright giddy. "Great! When can I see her? Is she okay? What about Piper?"

"There's no mention of medical treatment, so I would assume they are both in good health. As for your other friend, she is now listed as missing. I'm not sure what that means. The blast site has been thoroughly scanned and searched. Perhaps she was taken to a human hospital?"

"Maybe. You're sure there's no way she could still be at the stadium?" The idea of Piper being trapped under rubble, in pain and in the dark, made her stomach curdle.

"Our equipment is far more advanced than anything on your world. She isn't there."

She sighed. "Well, that's something. She's one of the feistiest women I've ever met. Whatever happened, she'll find a way home." She hoped like hell she was right. Aria had already lost her parents. Losing Piper would destroy her.

"May the Gods make it so."

"Aria is probably out of her mind with worry. I should go see her."

Torel's arm tightened around her and his jaw flexed. "Not now."

"You might be my mate, but you're not my master. You can't tell me what to do all the time, Tor."

"I'm not your master, but I am the one responsible for your wellbeing. You haven't rested enough today, and we'll be caught up in the Scorching again soon. We can go see her during our next respite."

"You're making sense, but I still don't want to wait."

"But you will, because as stubborn as you are, you know I'm right."

Torn between laughter and grumbling, she opted to laugh, though she didn't actually agree to stay in bed. He might be right, but she needed to see Aria.

He gathered her into his arms and rose from the chair in a display of strength that made her brain melt a little around the edges. He carried over to the freshly made bed and set her gently into the middle of it. "Get comfortable and try to get some sleep. I will join you soon."

The first stirrings of desire filled her, and she reached for him, grasping his hands and tugging him down onto the bed. "How about you join me now, instead?"

He gave in for a moment, kissing her with a fiery passion that made her heart race and her entire body ache with need. She'd always had a healthy libido, but when it came to Torel, she was insatiable. It had to be the Scorching. When it faded, all of this would fade, too. Once he was gone, it would be a wonderful memory, and that was all. That's how it had to be. Anything more would be a betrayal of her vows to Jeff.

When he ended the kiss and left the bed, she almost pouted. "Where are you off to?"

He crossed to the stretch of wall that concealed his closet and opened it with a wave of his hand. "I need to fetch a few things from my office. Research notes, mostly, but I should also check on the status of the high-risk patients while I'm in medical. I won't be long."

"I know it can't be easy being cooped up with me when you're used to working all the time." She shooed him toward the door. "If someone hadn't ordered me to rest, I'd be trying to get down some of the ideas I have for my new series of articles."

Torel dressed quickly and then headed for the door. "You'll sleep better if you close your eyes."

"I'll close them once you're gone. Right now, I'm enjoying the view."

He was gone seconds later, but not fast enough to hide the fact her comments made him blush.

She counted to thirty before getting out of bed. Once she was sure he wasn't coming back, she bounced over to the closet and grabbed one of the outfits he'd had made for her. She'd tried them all on already to make sure they fit, but this was the first time she'd actually worn one for more than a few seconds. The dress was a simple, flowing design, and the pale gold fabric complimented her skin tone nicely. Good thing, too, because she was going without makeup or any of her usual hair products.

Her hair had exploded into a riot of curls, but there wasn't a thing she could do about it. None of her belongings, including her purse, phone, and the clothes she'd been wearing, had survived the bombing.

"Computer, do you speak English?" she asked as she did her best to tame her hair.

"I do. What can I help you with?"

"I need to find a human woman – uh, female – onboard this ship. Can you do that?"

"Affirmative. Who do you wish to locate?"

"Aria Frasier."

"That female is currently located in the ship's nursery. Do you need directions?"

Yeah, there were definitely some appealing things about the Pyrosian lifestyle. Service droids, helpful computers that didn't tell you what to do or question your life choices…

"Directions would be great, thanks."

A minute later she was out the door and headed down the empty corridor at a run, muttering the directions repeatedly so she didn't forget them. The last thing she wanted to do was get lost. She rounded the last turn and careened into someone walking out a door.

"Sorry! I'm trying to find the nursery. Where is it?" The other woman turned to face her and Haley squealed in delight. "Oh my god. Aria? Is that you?"

"Haley?"

The two women stared at each other for a moment.

Aria looked good. In fact, she was glowing, and so were her eyes.

"You're mated to a Pyrosian?" Aria spoke first.

"And so are you! I'm glad you said yes." She couldn't believe that her oh so cautious friend had taken the plunge and accepted her match. As she spoke, a big, gruff looking Pyrosian stepped into view and headed straight for Aria.

She thought she recognized Tarjen from the photo, though the image hadn't done justice to the reality of the big, sexy alien. "Whoa, is that him? He's way cuter in person."

Aria blushed and beamed. It was the happiest Haley had seen her. After a brief round of introductions and a quick round of catch-up, Haley finally got to tell her friend what happened during the bombing. It wasn't easy to look Aria in the eye and admit that she was likely the reason Piper was missing. "Once the first bomb went off, we ran for it. She was behind me when we both got caught in a blast. Part of the stadium smacked me in the head, and that's all I remember. I'm sorry. I don't know where she is. No one seems to." Guilt rolled over her like a runaway Zamboni. "I should have made her go ahead. I wasn't able to run very fast in my heels, but she wouldn't leave me."

Aria shook her head. "It's not your fault."

Haley didn't believe that, and she was about to say so when Tarjen dropped a bombshell. "I think I know where Piper is. If I am correct, then she is safe."

She listened quietly as Aria and her mate spoke. It

was hard to believe what she was hearing, but Tarjen seemed entirely sincere. Apparently, Piper had taken up with another alien named Radek. And he was…a dragon? She started to giggle and couldn't stop, not even when Aria broke off to glare at her.

"This isn't funny!"

Haley finally got her laughter under control enough to reply. "Oh honey, it is. You just can't see it yet. Of all the men in the galaxy, only your sister could snag herself a damned *dragon*."

Aria ignored her and started peppering Tarjen with questions again, and the answers just kept getting more entertaining. Radek was an ice dragon, with scales and wings and a frosty breath weapon of some kind. Things were just getting interesting when both Aria and Tarjen looked past her, and a familiar voice rang through the air.

"Why is it you insist on defying my every instruction, *otama*? You are supposed to be in our quarters, resting before the Scorching takes hold again." Torel had found her.

"And I'll be there soon, but I had to find Aria." She turned to smile at Torel, who looked as if he'd caught her with her hand in a giant jar of cookies. "Torel, this is Aria. Aria, this is Torel, my, uh mate." She almost launched into an explanation of how this mating wasn't permanent, and she'd be going back to Earth in a few days, but now didn't seem to be the time. Aria was clearly going with Tarjen, which meant that pretty soon, she'd be losing her best friend to her new life.

Torel and Tarjen exchanged a few words of congratulations, and then Torel spun on his heel, pulled her close, and lifted her into his arms like she was a wayward child. "Say goodbye to your friend now. You are going back to bed, and this time I will personally see to it that you don't leave it again until I give you permission."

She stuck her tongue out at him. "You are not the boss of me. Mate, not master, remember?"

He didn't answer with words, he simply cocked an arrogant brow and growled low in his throat. Damn, she loved it when he did that.

She leaned back to wave at Aria. "I think we're going, now. We'll talk soon, and don't worry about Pi. That girl can take care of herself. I'll see you after this Scorching thing finally wears off. Bye!"

"I thought we agreed that you were staying in bed to rest?" Torel sounded equally amused and annoyed as he carried her back to his room.

"I agreed it was a good idea, but I really wanted to see Aria. She's my best friend, and I wanted to know she was okay. Did you get what you needed from your office?"

"I have what I need, yes. And I learned that Eva, the last human patient in our medical center, is finally recovering. I thought you'd like to know."

"I'm glad to hear it."

Torel continued. "Now you know that Aria is fine, will you promise me there'll be no more covert departures from our quarters?"

"I'll make you that promise if you make me one. You agree not to tell me to stay in bed if and when one of my friends needs me." She didn't acknowledge that he'd refer to his rooms as 'theirs,' or how much she liked hearing him say it.

"Agreed. And if you wish to go anywhere, I'd like to accompany you."

"You would? Why? Are there parts of this ship I shouldn't see?"

"You're welcome to see any part of the ship you wish. Once the Scorching is over, I'll give you a tour if you like."

Confusion struck. "I'd like that, but I don't understand why you'd want to accompany me if there's nothing I can't see."

He muttered something in Pyrosian and walked faster, glowering at a uniformed male who happened to be passing by.

"If you're going to grumble, could you do it in English?"

"I want to go with you because I don't like the way other males are looking at you. They should respect the fact you are a mated female, but some of them…"

"I've seen less than a dozen males since I left to find Aria, and that includes you and Tarjen. You have no reason to be jealous, Tor." She wasn't going to tell him she hadn't even noticed the other men. He was the only one she wanted, and that scared the hell out of her.

His expression turned stormy. "I'm not jealous. Well, I am, but it's not a choice. It's the Scorching."

"You sure?" She was goading him, and she didn't know why. Maybe because she wanted him to feel jealous. Wanted him to care about her, even if this wasn't going anywhere. This Scorching thing was messing with her head as well as her sex drive.

"I'M sure it is the Scorching that is making me act this way." Torel cradled Haley close to his chest and tried to calm himself as they approached the door to his quarters. He hadn't liked returning to an empty room. It felt wrong. As if someone had simultaneously turned up the gravity while dimming the lights. He hadn't needed to ask the computer where his errant mate had gone. He could sense her presence calling to him. The bond between them was getting stronger by the hour. Despite what he'd just told Haley, he wasn't sure his jealousy was entirely the fault of the Scorching. It felt more permanent than that.

He was starting to question if they would be able to go their separate ways when the Scorching ended. When he'd suggested it to her, he'd believed it would be a simple matter. But now he wasn't so sure. He needed to study their mating more, applying what he'd learned of human biology and how it was affected by Pyrosian genetics. That was why he'd gone to his office earlier. Some of the information he needed wasn't on any database, it was contained in antique books and handwritten notes from researchers long since gone from the world.

Haley was quiet until they got back to their quarters. It wasn't until he set her back on her feet near the bed that she spoke again. "Do you know anything about Romaki dragons?"

He stilled. "A little. Why? And where did you even hear of them?"

"Tarjen said that my friend Piper is most likely with one right now, which is why no one can find them. I have questions."

"I could try and answer your questions, but I think you'd get better information from the ship's database. All I really know is that there two clans, fire, and snow. They are isolated, and believe that to leave their planet would result in the loss of their..." He paused to remember the word he needed. "Their magic."

She inhaled sharply. "Magic is real?"

He snapped his fingers, summoning a small ball of bright flames. "Very real. There is no science that can explain this ability. It is a gift from the Gods."

"Right. I put the whole, 'you can summon fire' thing out of my mind. It's still hard for me to wrap my head around, you know?"

"It's strange for me, too, and I knew it would happen if I ever mated."

"Still trying to wrap my head around that little fact, too. I'm mated. To an alien from another planet." She moved in closer, setting her hand on his bicep and smiling up at him, her golden eyes glowing with desire, now. "And a very sexy mate, too. If you put out that fire of yours, Tor, I think we can start a different kind of fire in that nice, comfy bed of yours."

He closed his fist around the flame, snuffing it out. "I thought you wanted to know about the Romaki?"

"I do. Later. Right now, I can feel the Scorching starting to burn again, and I want to enjoy it while it lasts. My friends are okay. Your last human patient is going to recover. We don't have anything left to worry about. Which means we can relax and let go. The real world and all its worries will be waiting for us soon enough."

She was right. They had another cycle until the Scorching ended. By then, he might have created enough memories to last until the next time he came to Earth. Or maybe, it might give him enough time to find a way to tempt her to stay with him. He hadn't wanted a mate, but now that he'd met Haley, he wasn't sure he had the strength to keep his promise and let her go.

CHAPTER SIX

Haley roused from sleep grudgingly at first, but when she reached for Torel and only found an empty bed, she sat up fast and looked around in confusion. "Torel?"

He was always there when she woke, either asleep beside her, reading, or watching her with a look of wonder. She liked waking up like that. Liked it more than she cared to admit, in fact.

"I knew I shouldn't have set the lights so bright. I did not want to wake you. You need more sleep." Torel was standing near the bed, dressed in the same type of uniform she'd seen him in the first time they had met. The dark material was trimmed in red, and there were gold markings of some kind on his collar, as well as an insignia over his heart.

"You're kinda overdressed for someone who isn't allowed to be on duty," she said.

Torel moved in close and bent down to kiss her

forehead. "I've been called out for an emergency. I didn't want to wake you, but I left a note for when you woke up."

Sure enough, there was a data pad beside her pillow with a few words displayed on the screen.

"You should have woken me." Emergency or not, she didn't like the idea of him sneaking out of their bed. Even if it wasn't really theirs and this wasn't a permanent thing and she wasn't falling for him...*shit*. Guilt and denial washed over her, dousing her anger in an icy wave. Falling for Torel meant betraying Jeff's memory. She wouldn't do that. She couldn't.

Torel stood up and stepped back, his jaw set in a stubborn line she'd come to know too well. "It was my determination that you needed to sleep. I don't have time to discuss this with you right now." He turned on his heel and walked away.

"I hope you can save him."

He didn't look back, but as he passed through the door, she heard his answer. "So do I."

The feel of the room changed the second she was alone. It was too quiet, too empty, and even the temperature felt cooler, like Torel had taken all the warmth with him when he left. She rose from the bed and pulled on the first thing she found, which happened to be one of Torel's shirts. She breathed in his scent and immediately felt less alone. "Nope, no good."

If just catching Torel's scent was enough to affect her emotional state, she was in trouble. She stripped naked again and went to the closet to find something else to wear. She selected a pair of pants and a top from the items Torel had brought for her. They were made of a soft, thick, grey and red fabric that reminded her of well-worn flannel pajamas. *Perfect*.

Once she was dressed, she sat down in one of the chairs and stared out at Earth, trying to gather her thoughts. It wasn't easy. The Scorching was still making it hard to think clearly. She started by reminding herself where she belonged. It wasn't difficult to do when her planet was right in front of her, a blue and green jewel spinning in the dark expanse. "That's home," she reminded herself. "That's where your job is, your home, your family. That's where Jeff's buried."

Saying Jeff's name brought another flood of guilt. He was supposed to be the love of her life. The one she would spend forever with. How could that be true if she was also supposed to be Torel's mate? Hell, she didn't even know if they were mates. Not really. The sex was epic, and she liked spending time with Torel, but that was hardly confirmation she was supposed to be with him for the rest of her life.

She was supposed to have spent the rest of her life with Jeff. He was her rock, the only one who encouraged her to do more than what was expected of her. "I miss you," the words tumbled out before she could stop them, and so did the tears. "Dammit, if you hadn't died, none of this would be happening! You were supposed to stay with me. We made a promise to each other, and now you're gone, and I don't know what I'm supposed to do with my life!" She closed her eyes and clenched her fists against the rage and pain that had been part of her life every day since she'd buried Jeff. Tears scalded her face, but they didn't bring answers or peace.

When the emotional storm finally passed, she wiped her eyes, took several centering breaths, and went to the bathing room to find a cloth and cold water. If Torel saw her like this, he'd know something was wrong, and he was the last man in the world—or the galaxy – she wanted to talk to about her feelings. At least until she figured out what the hell her feelings were.

When she had repaired most of the damage, she wandered back to the main room, too restless to stay still and too tired to do much else. Pouring herself a glass of water, she headed back to her chair. "Computer, do you have anything on the Romaki Dragon Clans that is translated into English?"

"Nothing like that exists in my database. I can translate something for you, however."

"I just want to know the basics. How long will it take?"

"Only a few minutes. Would you like me to begin?"

"Please."

Since she had a little time, she sat in the chair Torel had used earlier and picked up one of the textbooks he'd brought back from his office. It was nothing but text, but she flipped through the pages anyway. Apart from a few symbols that marked the doors and panels on the ship, it was the first time she'd seen the Pyrosian language in written form. That got boring quickly, so she picked up one of his tablets and tapped the screen the same way she'd seen Torel do it. The tablet activated immediately, and she stared at the image on the screen. It was an anatomy diagram of a female. Most of the labels were in Pyrosian, but there were a few handwritten notes attached to the image, and some of them included words she recognized. Human. Female. Breeding. *What the hell?* She started reading, trying to make sense of what little she could make out. A few more flips and she found medical texts in English, along with more handwritten notes that were a mix of both languages. She still didn't understand everything, but she grasped enough to know what she was looking at. This was fertility and genetic research. Lots of it, along with a stack of information and notes about how the genetic matching worked, and how it might be increased to allow for more human women to be matched to Pyrosian males.

The computer announced it had translated her information on the Romaki, but instead of reading that, she continued, enlisting the computers' help to translate Torel's research. She expected it to refuse, or claim the work was classified, but instead the ship's computer merely complied with each request, providing printed copies of everything she asked for.

The more she read, the more she questioned everything Torel had told her. Were she and the other women being tricked somehow, convinced they were destined to love someone from another planet just to ensure the Pyrosian race survived? She hadn't been able to focus since meeting Torel--was that part of it, too? Was this the reason she was betraying her vows to Jeff and falling for someone she barely knew?

It made a terrible kind of sense.

TOREL WATCHED the bio-monitor and prayed to the Gods for a sign. A blip. A flutter. Any indication that Keth was responding to treatment. He had tried everything he knew and few more things that he'd invented on the fly, but so far, none of it had worked.

"I don't understand," Ista, his second in command, murmured as she stared at the readouts. They had moved Keth to one of the small private rooms so none of the other patients would know how serious things were. "There's no reason he shouldn't be awake. We've run every test twice, and there's nothing on any of the scans."

"My first mentor used to say that medicine can only do so much, the rest is up to the patient. If he wants to come back, he will."

Ista nodded. "If he doesn't…"

She didn't finish her sentence. It wasn't necessary. They both knew what would happen if he didn't recover. Eva was awake and already in the thrall of the Scorching. They were almost out of time to save them both. The bond was just too strong. His own bond was so powerful that even now, he couldn't go for more than a few seconds without thinking about Haley. If he focused, he could sense her presence. She was awake and unhappy, but there was nothing he could do about that right now. He had to focus on the problem in front of him, which was damned difficult when all he wanted was to think about her. Be with her. Hold her. He groaned. "By the flames, that's it! I am an *akinu* for not thinking of it sooner."

"Sir?" Ista gave him a confused look.

"Get his mate in here. Now."

To her credit, Ista didn't hesitate. She dashed back to the main room and seconds later she was issuing orders to the others.

Torel stayed where he was, still watching the monitors. "Don't give up your life spark, yet. Your mate needs you, Keth. Without you, she will suffer and likely die."

It only took a few minutes for Eva to arrive. She was on her feet, though Ista was beside her, helping her along. A medi-droid hovered nearby to monitor her bio-signs.

The moment Eva saw Keth, she gasped, crossed the room to his side, and then gripped his hand in hers. "He's the one that saved me? This is Keth? My…" she stumbled over her next word. "…mate?"

"He is. And now, we need you to save him," Torel said.

Eva looked up, frowning. "What can I do?"

"You're already doing it. Hold his hand. Tell him you're here. Talk to him."

"How's that going to save him?"

"You're his mate. The one he has waited his entire life to find. If there's anything that will keep him here, it's you." Every word he uttered made him regret how he'd handled things with Haley. He'd lied to himself, and to her, about their bond. She was his mate, and he had done everything he could to deny it. Instead of welcoming her, he'd pretended his life hadn't altered trajectory the moment she'd initiated the Spark.

Eva tentatively stroked Keth's cheek. "Hello, Keth. I'm Eva. You need to wake up, now. I'm alone on this ship, and I'm scared."

The monitor registered a fluctuation. It was tiny, but by the Flames of the First Ones, it was there! "He heard you. Keep talking to him."

Eva leaned over Keth, her blonde hair falling around her face as she lowered her head until she was next to his ear. Torel didn't hear what she said, but there was a flurry of activity on the monitors.

Both he and Ista watched in silent amazement as Eva singlehandedly did what they hadn't been able to do. Breath by breath, moment by moment, Keth was waking up.

"What made you think to bring her to be with our patient?" Ista asked.

"Haley."

His second in command nodded in understanding. "Kastor and I have been together for so long, I forgot how consuming the bond can be in the beginning. Speaking of your mate, I think you should return to her.

The emergency has passed. I'm officially taking you off-duty again."

He grinned. "You're enjoying your time in charge a little too much. Be careful, or when we get home, I'll recommend you for a command of your own."

Ista's eyes widened. "You would?"

"I would. You've more than proven yourself ready."

She beamed with pride as she pointed to the door. "Thank you. Now, go. You've been away from Haley too long as it is. She will be missing you."

"She understands why I had to leave. I'm just glad I'll be returning with good news." He wasn't about to admit to Ista that his mate hadn't been happy when he'd left. And judging by what he sensed from her at this moment, things hadn't improved while he was gone.

Despite Ista's instructions, he didn't rush back to his quarters. He needed a few moments to think about matters. Part of him wanted to continue believing that once the Scorching passed, he'd be able to return to his old life as if nothing had changed, even though he was coming to accept that wasn't going to happen. If he couldn't have his old life, what *did* he want?

The answer came too quickly. He wanted Haley. Not as a sexual partner he'd see once or twice a year, but part of his life. By the time he reached his door, he still hadn't come up with how to tell Haley he'd changed his mind. He went in any way. They were two, rational adult beings. They'd find a way to make this work.

Haley was dressed and sitting by the window, her

face screwed into a stormy scowl. The moment she heard him enter, she threw down the tablet she'd been reading and stood. "You want to explain to me what all this is?" She gestured to the table, which was strewn with his research and a stack of fresh printouts.

"It's my research, and uh, whatever you've had the computer print for you. What's wrong, *otama*? I sensed your unhappiness while I was gone, but I thought it was because I'd left you without an explanation."

"I've got news for you, Tor. I'm more than unhappy, I'm angry! I got bored and started looking through your research. Do you know what I found?"

"I would assume you found my notes and textbooks, all of which are written in Pyrosian." He had no idea why she was so angry, but something was seriously wrong. He wanted to fix this quickly so they could talk about what he'd realized while they were apart. "Why are you so angry?"

"Are you kidding me? Your research is all about how to turn human women into nothing more than brood mares for your breeding project." She waved a printout in front of her. "You even call them breeders!"

"I did no such thing," he retorted defensively.

"It says so right here." She raised the printout higher and then screamed. The paper burst into flames.

He was at her side in a second, but by then the paper was reduced to ash. Her hand, however, was still covered in flames.

"Make it stop. Make it stop!" She flailed her arm helplessly.

"You are the only one who can do that. Calm your mind." Apparently, his mate could control fire after all. This fact would only add to his argument that she belonged with him, on Pyros.

"Calm my—are you fucking kidding me? I'm on fire!"

"And you will be until you calm yourself. Close your eyes and visualize the flames growing smaller and then vanishing. If it helps, close your fist as you do it, as if you were extinguishing them that way."

She stilled and closed her eyes. After a few seconds, the flames were gone.

"Well done."

"I better not be," she snapped and opened her eyes. She drew her hand in close and examined it carefully.

"Your flames will never harm you. That's part of the magic."

She lowered her hand and glowered at him. "You did this to me! First, it was sparks and sex and now it's mates, magical freaking flames and breeding plans! I'm not doing this. Not any of it. In fact, once I get back to Earth, I'm going to tell everyone what you're really up to. I saw your notes. You're trying to find ways to turn more human women into baby factories so you can save your race, and to hell with what we human women want!"

"You've misunderstood. Sit down and we'll talk about this."

She shook her head wildly. "No. No more talking. I

want to see my friend, and then we are getting out of here."

"You can't leave. We're mated. I learned today that if we're separated, it will be hard on both of us. I don't want you to leave, Haley." He reached for her, but she moved away. He could sense her emotions more clearly now, and they were a seething tangle of fear, anger, and...guilt? He didn't understand. What was she feeling guilty about?

"Right. And you only just realized this? Yesterday it was fine for us to hook up and then move on, but now, suddenly, we can't? That's awfully convenient."

His legendary control shattered, and his next words came out as a shout. "No, it's not! I didn't want this any more than you did. Remember?"

"How can I trust anything you've said after what I've read? I was going to honour Jeff's memory and stay single. I wasn't ever going to let my heart get crushed again. Then you come along and the next thing I know we're...we're..." she threw her hands in the air. "I don't even know what the hell we are."

"We're true mates. A divine match. I didn't understand what that meant at first, but I just saw Eva bring her mate back from the brink of death simply by speaking to him. We were meant to be together forever, not living on opposite sides of the galaxy."

"I'm not going to let you take me away from my home and my friends."

He blew out a frustrated breath. "Your friends are

mated to a Pyrosian and a Romaki. If you go back to Earth, then you'll be going alone."

"Not once I tell them the truth."

"You don't know what the truth is. If you'd just sit down and let me explain, we could get this sorted out."

"I know what I read."

"You read a translation of complex medical jargon and abbreviated notations done by a computer that is not programmed for that kind of task. Now, sit down and let me explain."

She folded her arms over her chest and glared. "Don't you dare bark orders at me right now. Sexy play time is over."

"It's only over until the next time the Scorching hits. We've not finished the cycle, yet."

"Oh, yes we are." She threw out an arm and pointed to the door. "We're very finished. And since I don't have anywhere to go right now, I'm asking you to leave. I'll let you know when I've spoken to Aria and I'm ready to leave the ship."

"You're not leaving. If you leave, we'll both suffer," he was so frustrated he almost snarled the words.

She waved her hands in the air in front of her, highly agitated. "I don't know if I believe that. I can't talk to you right now. Just go!"

The last thing he wanted was to leave Haley alone. He needed to fix this. To explain. To make her understand how wrong she was. He just didn't know how. Not yet. "Alright, I'll go for now, but I will be back when you are calmer."

She pressed her lips together in a tight line and frowned. "Hmph. Free piece of advice for future reference. Nine times out of ten, telling a human woman to calm down will have the exact opposite effect."

"I wasn't…" He didn't bother finishing his sentence. There was no point.

CHAPTER SEVEN

H~ALEY~ ~STORMED~ over to the bed and dropped onto it with enough force she bounced. "Fuck!"

She hadn't meant for things to get so out of control. She certainly hadn't planned on talking about her feelings, or yelling, but everything had kind of exploded out of her -- including actual flames. That had been the last straw. The end of her ability to cope with anything else.

It didn't excuse what she'd done, though. She'd accused Torel of lying to her, and now that she'd said it aloud, it didn't feel right. She'd let her emotions run rampant, and that was never a good idea. Hell, in the past hour she'd broken just about every rule of journalism. Don't get emotionally involved. Don't make assumptions. Double check all your facts, and always get both sides of a story.

Her emotions were still bubbling over in a messy froth that made it impossible for her to think straight.

One of the things she'd learned during her grief counselling sessions was to never make important decisions when emotional. It was time she followed that advice.

"I really hope he doesn't come back and see me tied up like a pretzel," she muttered as she sat up, folded her legs into the half lotus position, and set her hands atop her thighs, palms up. Once she was comfortable, she closed her eyes and tried to remember the breathing technique Aria had taught her during their sessions.

It took time to recall the pattern, and much longer to actually start to feel centered. By the time she was clearheaded again, some of the tension had left her body, and she paused to flex her shoulders and roll her head from side to side. Once she was relatively calm, she started working through her feelings, untangling them bit by bit. Anger at the idea Torel might have tricked her. Guilt about how she felt about her sexy alien match. Then there was the issue of what the hell she actually felt for Torel. Was it lust, or something more? Was it even real? What was she going to do if it *was* real?

She started to tense up and ended up going through the whole breathing thing again. She still felt silly, but like Aria always told her, you have to go with what works. "I'd feel better if I could talk to Aria about all this," she mused aloud.

"Are you referring to the same Aria Frasier you wished me to locate earlier?" The computer's query startled her.

"Uh, yeah. I am."

"Would you like me to enable communications with her?"

She started to nod vigorously, then realized the computer needed a verbal response. "Hell, yes I'd like you to do that."

"Sending a communication request, now."

Before she had time to ask any other questions, the request went through and Aria's face appeared on a monitor a few feet away from the bed. "Hi, Haley. Everything ok—shit. Clearly not. Why are you crying? And where's Torel? Wait, is he the reason you're crying?"

"No, everything is not okay. I'm not crying. Well, I was, but I stopped. I threw Tor out of his room, I uh, have no idea where he went. And to answer your last question, yes, he's part of the reason I'm upset. Also, I set some paper on fire. And my arm. Turns out, I got the full Pyrosian freak package. Think I can get a job as a superhero when I get home? Girl of Flame? Captain Firestarter?"

"Home?" Aria frowned. "You're going home? And what's this about setting things on fire? Are you okay?"

"I'm fine." She held up her hand. "No burns, see? I have no idea how I'm going to explain the gold eyes and new party trick to my parents, though. They're going to lose their minds."

"Probably," Aria agreed. "But why are you planning on going back to Earth? Is Torel staying, too?"

"Torel's not staying. At least, he hasn't said anything

about it. I'm going back because I don't think this is going to work, and well, I don't think I can trust him."

"Why not?" Aria asked in a tone Haley hadn't heard in a long time. Aria was in counselor mode, asking probing questions without judgement or comment.

"Torel and I only went through with this mating thing because we didn't really have a choice. He promised me that once it was over, I was free to go home if that's what I wanted." She paused, then mentally cursed herself for a fool. She really had let her emotions get in the way of following the facts. She should have remembered that. It threw a big wrench into her theory that Tor and the others were tricking women into going back to Pyros with them. He'd told her he didn't want her to leave, but he never once said she couldn't.

"Is that what you want?"

"I don't know. Torel had to leave for a couple of hours today, and while he was gone, I got bored and started looking around for something to do."

"What did you find?" Aria asked.

"Torel's research. He left it in our—his room. I started flipping through it. I couldn't read any of it, but I got the ship's computer to translate it for me." She took a breath, not sure how to tell Aria what she'd discovered. "Did you know that the Pyrosians are studying human fertility and genetics? They're even trying to find ways to manipulate our genetics to match more of us to their unclaimed males. Having read all that, I don't know if I can trust Torel anymore."

Aria pursed her lips in thought, then asked, "What did Torel say when you asked him about all this?"

Trust Aria to go straight for the question Haley didn't want to answer. She twisted a lock of hair around her finger and sighed. "I might have hit him with a full broadside when he came back."

Aria's lips twitched a little. "How so?"

"I kind of accused him of plotting against humanity, and uh, that was the moment I lit up like a torch," she confessed.

"You must have been very upset. That's what happened to Gwen, too. She got angry, and that's when her ability manifested."

"Gwen? Spokeswoman for the Star-Crossed Dating Agency, that Gwen?"

"Yes. Did you know she's got a little girl almost the same age as Melody?"

"You've spoken to other women? Are they happy? Do they know about the breeding plan they're part of?"

"I've met with Princess Maggie, Gwen, and their friend, Lisa, and yes, they're happy. I had doubts of my own, and they helped me work through some of them. In fact, I had just left them when I ran into you."

Well, that shot another hole in her theory. "I was so sure…"

Aria's expression softened. "I know. But what you're saying doesn't match with what I was told, or what I've seen. Believe me, these ladies aren't the kind who would just agree to something like that. They're smart, independent women who are very much in love with their mates."

Shit. She sighed heavily as logic finally won over her suspicions. "I think I might owe Torel an apology. Or at the very least, a chance to explain. He asked for that, but I wasn't in any mood to hear him out."

"Do you know why you were so ready to believe the worst?" Aria asked.

"Not really."

Her friend just stared at her in silence.

"Okay, maybe I have some idea," she finally admitted.

Aria just continued to look at her, waiting.

"It's about Jeff." She threw her hands up in frustration. "Everything always seems to come back to him in the end."

"How long has he been gone?"

"Three years. You know that."

"So, why do you think you haven't let yourself move on? Why does everything 'come back to him,' to use your words?"

"Because he was my husband, and I swore to love him forever. He was my soulmate."

"And now you're being told you're destined to be with someone else. That can't be easy to reconcile."

"It's not! People don't get two soulmates, that's not how it works."

"Who made that rule?" Aria asked.

"I, uh. I don't know."

"People lose the ones they love every day. It doesn't

mean they never get to be in love again." She smiled gently and threw her words back at her. "That's not how it works."

"But Jeff and I were a team. We were going to change the world. Tackling injustice and holding the ones in power accountable for their decisions. We were an unstoppable team…and then the cancer came and we weren't unstoppable anymore."

"I know. But Jeff didn't want you to stop trying, did he?"

"No, but I didn't know how to do it alone. I…I gave up." The confession hurt. She'd known what she was doing for a while, now, but knowing it and naming it weren't the same thing.

"You didn't give up, you just put everything on pause."

Now she'd admitted the truth, she didn't bother trying to dress it up. "Three years isn't a pause, it's a choice." Especially since during that time, she'd reverted back to the person she'd been before meeting Jeff. Returning to the family business, trying to appease her parents, focusing on work instead of living any kind of life.

"Let's call it a non-choice. A holding pattern," Aria said.

"Okay."

Aria leaned toward the screen. "Are you ready to step back into the fray again and restart your life?"

She thought about that for a few minutes, pushing

aside her fears and doubts to get to the real answer buried beneath. "I think I am, yeah."

"Then the question you need to ask yourself is this. What does that life look like?"

Haley started to answer, but Aria put up her hand and shook her head. "Take some time and be sure of what you want before you answer. We're standing on the brink of some seriously big changes."

"You got that right. None of us had any idea how much was going to change when Piper came bursting into your kitchen that night. Speaking of Piper, have you heard from her? Is she okay?"

Aria beamed. "They found them. I was just about to contact you to let you know when you messaged me. She's fine. So's the alien dragon-dude who flew off with her." She frowned. "I still don't know how I feel about him. The man did abscond with my sister…" she shook her head. "It's going to take me some time to process."

"Yeah, I bet. But he's bringing her home, safe and sound. That has to count for something."

"It does. They're coming back to the ship later today. We're going to meet the shuttle when it arrives. Want to join us?"

"I wish I could, but I suspect by then Torel and I will be either having angry, Scorch-driven break up sex, or happy, Scorch-enhanced makeup sex."

"Scorch driven? Are you still feeling the effects of that? I thought it only lasted two days?"

"It does. I didn't meet Torel until I woke up in the medical center yesterday."

"Well, that explains why you're feeling everything so deeply right now. The mating fever made me so crazy that on day two I stormed out of Tarjen's room with Melody in my arms and no idea where I was going to go next."

Aria was the most level-headed, centered person she knew. If the Scorching had made her act like that… "That actually makes me feel a little better. Thanks. And thank you for talking me through this. I think I can work the rest out on my own, now."

"Good. I've been waiting for this day to come. I'm glad I could help."

"Yeah, yeah. You're very smart. And a good friend." She raised her hand to wave to Aria. "Talk later?"

"You bet." Aria disconnected first, which was probably a good thing since Haley had no idea how to end the call without asking the computer for help.

Once she was alone, she went through her breathing exercises for a third time. She needed to be clearheaded before she made any more decisions. As she breathed, though, something else started to affect her. Emotions that weren't her own slid around the periphery of her awareness, like shadows at the outer circle of a campfire.

As the minutes passed, the feelings got stronger. Frustration, confusion, and other emotions too complex to decipher. She focused on the feelings, then gasped as she finally understood what was happening. *Torel.* She was experiencing the bond he'd told her about, and it was more intense than she had imagined.

She closed her eyes and tried to take in everything she was experiencing. It was quickly evident that despite her earlier suspicions, this was no trick accomplished with hormones or alien technology. It wasn't part of some ruse to convince her and the other human women to stay with their mates. She was connected to Torel. She could *feel* him.

"How did he think this was going to be nothing more than an intergalactic friends with benefits scenario? He's in my *head*!" She rubbed her brow as if it would somehow quiet the emotional noise pouring into her brain. That was when she remembered what he told her when he'd come back from the medical center. He didn't want her to leave, because it would be hard on them both. She had been too angry to listen to him then. She'd even accused him of making it up.

She huffed in frustration, then got off the bed and started pacing. Every time she passed the stack of printouts and reports, she felt a twinge of regret. Torel had done nothing to deserve her distrust. He'd been honest and attentive from almost the first moment they'd found themselves thrust together. He never pushed her into anything she didn't want to do, and there was no denying the chemistry between them was off the damned charts. She started another lap of the room, but this time she paused at the window to look down at Earth. *What's left for me down there?*

The truth hit her like a slap in the face. There was nothing for her back home. She hadn't led much of a life since Jeff's death. Aria, Melody, and Piper were leaving. She could walk away from her apartment and her job in a second. Her parents would take a little longer. Maybe two minutes to say goodbye, and at least one of those minutes would be taken up with disapproving stares and bitter sighs of disappointment. Jeff's grave might be down there, but he wasn't there anymore. He had moved on to the next adventure. It was time she did the same.

"If I do that, what adventure do I want to move on to?" She lifted her gaze from the planet to the myriad of stars that gleamed in the darkness of space. Even as she stared into the void, she could feel Torel's presence in her mind. If she went with him, she'd have a partner again. Someone who challenged her and made her laugh. He wasn't carefree and wild like Jeff, but he was passionate about the things that mattered to him. She could feel enough of his emotions to know she was one of the things he cared about. When she looked past her fears and guilt, she felt the same way about him. It wasn't love. Not yet, anyway. But it was more than she ever imagined she'd feel for anyone ever again.

It didn't take long to make up her mind. There were no guarantees in life. Love and happiness weren't certainties, but she wasn't going to find either one if she didn't take this chance. Jeff had taught her life was all about taking risks. Wherever he was right now, she hoped he'd be proud of her for taking this one.

She turned from the window and headed for the door. She needed to find Torel, apologize, and tell him she'd made a decision.

CHAPTER EIGHT

Torel had read enough documentation on the mating bond to know how to temporarily mute the connection between himself and Haley: liquor. It had taken two drinks to start working, but he was finally free of it, at least for now. It wouldn't stop the Scorching from returning, though. Soon, he'd have to face Haley again, and he had no idea how to make her understand how wrong he'd been about their bond, and how much he wanted her to stay. He also needed to convince her there was no nefarious plot to trick any female into going back to Pyros. Until he figured how to do all that, he was staying in the officers' lounge, comfortably ensconced at the end of the bar. The servo-droid kept his glass full, the lounge was almost empty, and he had relative silence to come up with a plan.

The silence was broken when a familiar voice sounded from behind him. "I'd call you out for drinking while on duty, but I happen to know you're not supposed to be *on* duty right now, so what's with the uniform?" Commander Kash Denza appeared to his right. He was out of uniform and smiling, something he did a lot more of since he'd found his mate and accepted the mating bond.

"I got called in for an emergency. Keth wasn't reviving from stasis, and it was looking like he might not survive."

"I heard he's awake now, though. No one told me that was your doing." Kash gestured around them, his sweeping hand taking in everything from the lone droid serving drinks, to the near empty room, and the vista of stars visible outside the viewports. "It also doesn't explain why you're here, drinking instead of spending time with your mate."

"She's not pleased with me right now. She uh, requested I leave our quarters."

Kash tried, and failed, to suppress a chuckle as he took the seat next to Torel. "Things not going well?"

Torel drained his glass. "She read my research notes while I was away, and when I returned, she accused me, and all of Pyros, of lying to her people. She thinks we want to use the human females as breeders."

"Did you explain? Where the flames did she even get such a notion?" Kash stared at him. "What was in those notes of yours?"

"She didn't give me a chance to explain. Haley can't read Pyrosian, so she had the ship's computer translate. I believe the computer wasn't up to the task and made some errors. While she was expressing her outrage, she became sufficiently upset that she triggered her ability to summon fire, and after that…" Torel shrugged and gestured for the droid to refill his glass.

Kash burst out laughing. "I remember how that went for Gwen and me. At least there were no fire alarms triggered this time, and no one was doused in foam. I would have gotten a report if that had happened."

"How did you convince Gwen to stay after that happened? I was there, I saw how unhappy she was. Haley is angry right now, and I have no idea how to make her listen."

Kash shook his head. "The first thing you need to understand is that you can't make her do anything. You and I are used to giving orders and having them obeyed without question. That isn't going to happen with your mate. Flames, Joran's heir to the throne and not even he can tell Maggie what to do."

"They really aren't like Pyrosian females, are they?"

This time, Kash laughed so hard a small group of officers at the far side of the room turned to look over at them. "They're exactly like our females. Do you think your second in command would blindly obey her mate? I know my mother doesn't. My father might command armies and have the ear of the king himself, but he wouldn't dare try and order my mother around, and she'd set the house on fire if he tried."

"Then why don't the males matched to Pyrosian females have these problems?"

"Because our females know what will happen when

they meet their true mates. It's part of our culture, taught to both male and female younglings in the learning centers and in everyday life. Human cultures are very different. They are far more diverse, and none of them have anything like the Scorching."

None of this was news to him, but somehow, having Kash say it aloud helped put things in perspective. Torel stared into his drink and muttered, "You didn't used to be this socially aware."

"My mate has taught me a great deal. After witnessing some of the challenges that arose with this new round of matches, she suggested we teach our males even more about human culture. She also wants to us to be more open about the Scorching and all that it entails. The princess agrees with her."

"If that's the case, then the next group to come here will no doubt be better informed, as will the humans."

Kash sighed. "We're not coming back here for a while. It's too dangerous. The ones who attacked the Gathering are either dead or captured, but their leaders have not been found, yet. Until we can be sure it's safe, there will be no more Gatherings."

"Flames. I told Haley that if she wished, she could return to Earth, and I would visit her during our next Gathering. Are you telling me that isn't going to happen? She's going to think I lied to her about that, too."

"How can that be?" Kash asked, perplexed. "You're linked, aren't you? Even if the link is weak, she should be able to sense when you are telling the truth."

"The link is one-sided. I have been able to sense her for some time now, but she cannot sense me. At first, I hoped it was a sign our bond was weak enough we could continue on as if we were never mated. The only reason she agreed to any of this was because I promised her it didn't have to permanent."

"If she manifested her ability to manipulate fire today, maybe the bond was slow to develop, too?" Kash shrugged his big shoulders. "This is your field, not mine.

"Maybe. It's another area I need to study. There's so much we don't know about the humans and how they react to the activation of their Pyrosian genes."

"Worry about your research later. For now, you need to focus on your mate. Your bond is strong, right? How's she feeling? Is she calmer?"

Torel pointed to his half-empty glass. "I have no idea. Alcohol suppresses the link. Her anger and guilt were making it impossible for me to think clearly."

Kash pushed Torel's glass out of reach. "So that's why you're drinking. The liquor isn't helping you think clearly, though."

"True," Torel agreed. "And I'm running out of time to think of a plan to win her over."

Kash glanced behind him and grinned. "You're right. In fact, I'd say your time is up." He rose from his chair and clapped Torel on the shoulder. "Remember, you can't make her do anything, but you can tell her what you want, and why. Don't forget the why."

Torel turned and spotted Haley coming towards

him. Her eyes were red and swollen from crying, and he damned himself a fool for leaving her alone, even if that was what she'd asked him to do. If they got through this, if he found a way to convince her to stay with him, he would do better in future.

Kash called to the handful of officers still in the lounge as he walked. "All of you, come with me. The lounge is closed for the next hour. Take your drinks." As the others scrambled to their feet, he leaned in and said something to Haley in a voice pitched too low to hear. Whatever the commander said, it made her smile for a moment before she squared her shoulders and marched over to Torel.

In the brief seconds he had before she reached him, he rose to his feet and sent a silent prayer to the Gods for help. He would need it.

***

HALEY WALKED through the door into some sort of recreational area. The walls were painted a deep burgundy, with mosaic-like patterns breaking up the straight stretches of colour here and there. There were tables and chairs for several dozen beings, though only a single table was in use at the moment. There were large viewports, like the one in Torel's quarters, set into the far wall, and to her left was a long sweep of counter with a droid operating behind it. Two men were at the counter. One was Torel, and the other was a hulking bruiser of a man with a scarred face. He said something to Torel, laughed and then came straight towards her. As he moved, he started barking orders in Pyrosian to the handful of crewmembers in the room. She didn't know what he said, but it got the others moving fast.

She wasn't sure what this big male wanted, but as he got closer, he gave her a lopsided smile, then leaned in close and spoke in almost unaccented English. "Torel's a good male, and he cares deeply for you. I hope you two can work it out, but if not, try not to set the place on fire, okay?"

"I'll do my best, but I make no promises."

His smile broadened. "You sound like my Gwen. I annoyed her so much she set fire to our quarters the first time her powers manifested. We worked through our differences then. I hope you can do the same."

She offered him a hopeful smile. "So do I."

He nodded and moved on. A few seconds later, she and Torel were alone.

He was on his feet by the time she reached him, and the moment she was in range, he reached for her, then stopped. "May I?"

She closed the gap between them in a single leap, wrapping her arms around his shoulders and squeezing him tight. "Yes."

"This is a better reception than I expected." He folded her into his arms and buried his face in her hair.

"I'm sorry I didn't listen to you before. I get it now. The bond finally kicked in for me."

"It did?" His voice was so full of hope it made her heart swell. "So, if I swore to you that I am not trying to use your race as breeders, you'd know I was telling the truth?"

"I can do that? How?"

He stroked a hand down her back, pulling her in closer. "You can. Just close your eyes and focus on the bond while I speak. I'll show you the difference by telling you a lie, first."

"Okay."

"I want you to go back to Earth instead of staying with me."

She immediately felt the disconnect between his words and his emotions, followed by the impact of what he was telling her.

"You want me to stay?"

"He lifted his head and cupped a hand under her chin, lifting her head so their gazes met. "I do." She could feel the truth of his statement resonate deep in her heart.

"And you swear to me there's no trickery or coercion going on?"

"There's no trickery. No plot. No one is being used as a breeder. What you read was a bad translation of my notes. If you wish, I'll arrange for you to have the cognitive upgrade, so you can speak and write Pyrosian. Then you'll be able to understand my notes yourself…though I make no promises about my handwriting."

There was no sign of deception, not even the slightest disconnect. She breathed a sigh of relief. This bonding thing had its advantages. "I believe you."

"Thank the Gods."

"I'm not sure we should be thanking them, yet. They haven't exactly been gentle with us."

"They have not," he agreed. His thumb stroked over her cheek, and then he bowed his head to kiss her. It was a tender kiss, slow and sweet and full of promise, and as his mouth claimed hers, she could feel his emotions, too. It was even more intoxicating than the raw need of the Scorching. She kissed him back, craving the comfort of his touch and this time she knew it was more than hormones fueling her desire.

It was Torel who broke the kiss first, lifting his head with obvious reluctance. "Before we do that again, there's something else I need to tell you."

"Good or bad?" she asked.

"That depends on whether you decide to stay on Earth. When I told you I could come and visit whenever we returned for another Gathering, I didn't know my prince and his advisors had decided there will not be any more Gatherings until the danger passes."

The decision wasn't surprising. If she'd been thinking clearly, she would have come to the same conclusion. Her people needed more time and more information about their new allies, and even then, there would be those who feared change too much to ever accept their new reality. "So, if I go with you, I won't be coming back for a while?"

"It would be best to assume so," he replied, then blinked, his mouth falling open. "You're considering going with me?"

His reaction flowed through her, a heady mix of confusion and delight. "I am. In case you haven't sensed it yet, I care about you, Tor. That's really why I was so uh, volatile earlier. I loved my husband deeply, and when he died, I swore I would never let myself be hurt like that again. Then you came along and...I was scared and confused."

"I care about you, too." His expression turned sheepish. "I should make another confession, now. I may have imbibed enough liquor to temporarily suppress the link between us."

"You drowned me out with booze? Why?"

"I could feel your anger, fear, and hurt. I shouldn't have left you when you were feeling that way, but you ordered me to go. It was the only way I could give you the space you requested. Feeling your pain made me want to go to you, and that's not what you wanted." He kissed her again. "Besides, I needed time to make a plan and find a way to get you to stay with me."

"Did you come up with one?"

"Not really. All I know is how I feel about you, my *otama*. You are the brightest star in my sky, the one my life will orbit around forever. I don't know how to go back to the way I was before we met. I'm not even sure I can." He touched his chest, over his heart. "You're part of me, now."

"And you're part of me." She placed her hand over his. "I don't think we can go back, even if we wanted to."

"If you come with me, I will do my best to ensure you never regret your choice," he vowed.

"I'm sure we're going to have moments both of us question our choices. I don't know what the future will bring, but I do know this: I'd rather take my chances on a future with you than to face a life without you in it."

He nodded and then uttered something in Pyrosian, every word accompanied by a powerful swell of emotions. When he was done, he spoke again, this time in English. "I vow, by the Flames of the First One, to protect my mate from all who would do her harm. She will be my beloved, my lover, and my most cherished companion from now until we return to the Flame that birthed us."

There was a lump in her throat and tears in her eyes by the time he finished. Not only because the words were beautiful, but because she knew he meant every syllable.

"Until we return to the Flame that birthed us," she said, staring up into his golden eyes.

He growled her name, his fingers spearing into her hair as he kissed long and hard. The fires of the Scorching roared back to life, searing them both. He lifted her off her feet, his tongue plunging into her mouth to twine with hers. He walked away from the bar, and the next thing she knew he set her down in an empty space near the outer wall with one of the larger viewports at his back.

"Aren't we going back to our room?" she asked.

"That would take too long." He gripped the collar of

her shirt and tore it, baring her to the waist in one toe-curlingly sexy move.

"But the door locks."

"So does this one. Computer, lock the door to the officer's lounge and dim the lights by eighty percent."

"Those orders require a security override," the computer informed him.

He snarled several words in Pyrosian and the computer complied. When the lights went out, the view went from beautiful to breathtaking.

It was nighttime on whatever continent was currently racing by beneath them, though she could still pick out glowing constellations and rivers of light marking the various cities they flew over. In the distance, ribbons of blue and green light danced, filling the room with an ever-changing kaleidoscope of colours that flickered across her bare skin like a living rainbow.

she cooed in delight at the spectacle. "So beautiful."

He didn't even look out the window. His eyes never left her as he started stripping off the rest of her clothes. "Yes, you are."

When she was naked, he started on his own clothes, but when she tried to help he shook his head and moved around behind her. "You stay right where you are and enjoy the view."

"I think I'd rather see you right now."

"And you will, soon. Right now, I'm enjoying my view too much to move." His voice was low and husky with need, a need she could feel with an intensity that made her nipples tighten and her pussy slicken in anticipation of what was to come. He moved up behind her, caressing her from belly to breast. She could see their reflections in the window, the two of them little more than shadowy outlines filled with light and crowned by stars.

His gaze met hers through their reflection. "The first time you touched me, I thought that Spark meant I was about to lose everything I valued in life. I was wrong, *otama*. I haven't lost, I've gained."

She reached back to caress his cheek. "I believed I could only have one chance at happiness, and I lost it when Jeff died. I was wrong, too. I believe I can be happy again, but only if I'm with you. The link between us is too strong to deny."

He moved his hands to her shoulders and turned her, so she was facing him, then gathered her back into his arms. His mouth found hers, kissing her with so much fire it made her blood burn. The Scorching swept through her, hotter than a plasma torch and brighter than the sun.

"I cannot promise you a perfect life, but I will promise you this – I will do all I can to ensure that every day we have together has more happiness than tears." He whispered the words against her lips.

"You've got yourself a deal."

She kissed his mouth once more, then started working her way down his body, kissing and tasting him an inch at a time until she was kneeling at his feet. He set one hand on the crown of her hair but didn't try to move her closer.

"Haley, you don't—"

She didn't let him finish his sentence. She leaned forwards, gripping his cock with one hand as she took him into her mouth and hummed softly.

"Flames!" His threw back his head and groaned as she stroked his length with her tongue. When she hollowed her cheeks and sucked, his hand started to tremble, and his fingers tightened in her hair. She pulled back until her lips encircled the crown of his cock, then ran the tip of her tongue across one of the sensitive spots she'd discovered in their time together.

He started to rock his hips and she opened her mouth wide, running her tongue over the underside of his dick with each thrust he made. She loved pushing him beyond his limits, breaking his control with nothing more than her mouth and hands. When he growled her name, she took him all the way to the back of her throat and hummed a few victorious notes before releasing him.

"I was an *akinu* to think I could walk away from you," he said, helping her back to her feet.

"If that means some kind of fool, then I think that term applies to us both."

He kissed her quickly all while guiding her backwards until she was pressed against the cold, smooth surface of the window. He moved in close, trapping his hard length between them.

"I'd ask if anyone could see us right now, but I guess they'd need a spaceship or a telescope to make that happen."

"No one can see us. I will never share the glory of your body with anyone else," he paused his kisses just long enough to reply before bowing his head and claiming her mouth again.

He slid his hands slowly down her flanks to her hips, then bent down to cup her ass. "Hold on."

She gripped his shoulders, nodded, and then he lifted her high enough she could twine her legs around his waist. They came together perfectly, the two of them becoming one with a single motion that stole her breath and made her see stars of a very different kind than the ones outside. He buried himself to the hilt inside her, the moment made all the sweeter because she could sense his emotions as well as his body.

"I can feel you," she whispered. "All of you."

"And you always will." He punctuated his words with a hard thrust, and then there were no more words left to be spoken.

Her inner walls clenched around his cock, gripping him tight as they came together in a firestorm of desire. He lifted her higher, using the space between their bodies to pound into her in a bruising rhythm. Both of them surrendered to the Scorching, grinding and thrusting against each other in a mad race to the finish. He was out of control, relentless, and hungry, every kiss and touch hot enough to brand her flesh and mark her as his own.

"*Tokee*-- mine!" the words exploded out of him in a single breath.

She laughed, her nails raking his back. "Gods help you, yes I am."

His cock swelled inside her, pressing against her g-spot and pushing her to the brink of orgasm. She buried her face in the crook of his neck, muffling her cries of pleasure as she tumbled over the edge into ecstasy. He came seconds later, emptying himself inside her for what felt like forever.

"How is it that when I'm with you, I have no control?" he asked some time later.

"Don't blame me," she teased him. "Your Gods did this to you, remember?"

"Indeed they did." He raised his head and rubbed his bearded cheek against hers. "I'll have to thank them for that. I suspect my mother will be offering them prayers of thanks for the rest of her days."

She stiffened at the mention of his family. "They're going to be okay with this, right? I'm not exactly what your parents were expecting."

"You are my true mate. They will welcome you into the family and likely tell you every embarrassing story about me they know." He stepped away from the window, easing out of her body, then set her down with care.

"I'm not really good with in-laws. Jeff's parents didn't understand their son very well, and that made it hard for them to accept me."

"Different rules this time," he reminded her as he gathered up their clothes.

"Yeah, I imagine there's a lot less friction when you

can just blame your Gods if you don't approve of your kid's mate."

"You have to admit, our system does have a few advantages." Torel set their clothes down on a nearby table and walked, still naked, over to the bar, moved the service droid aside, and, retrieved several squares of fabric from a cubby beneath the counter.

"Maybe, but if we were at my place, we wouldn't have just gotten all wicked and wanton in front of a droid. Tell me those things don't have any capacity to record, or I'm going to have to dismantle that one, set the bits on fire, then chuck the ash out an airlock."

"I've already seen to it." He returned with the clothes, which he used to clean them both up before they got dressed.

They managed to tie the remains of her shirt together into something passable and slipped out into the corridor hand in hand and smiling. They still had challenges ahead of them, but Haley knew she'd made the right choice. Aria had asked her what she wanted her new life to look like. The answer was clear to her, now. Her future looked like Torel Zinn, her soulmate.

EPILOGUE

TOREL WAS DISCOVERING that life with a bright, curious partner had advantages he'd never considered. He was back in his favourite chair reading over his notes, but this time he had Haley in his lap and they were reviewing the information together. It had started because he wanted to show her where the computer's translation errors occurred, but they had continued because her questions and insights brought the data into focus in new ways and helped to raise new avenues for him to explore.

"I don't understand something, though. If your people have been to Earth before, why isn't here any record of it? A glyph, or a scroll, or even a legend? And where is the vessel they arrived in? I can accept that somehow there's no surviving record of your people's arrival, but how have we missed finding a spaceship? Those things aren't small."

"That's a mystery we might never solve, though

there are two competing theories that both make sense. The first is that the ship crashed, and the survivors found a way to destroy all traces of their existence so they could blend in without affecting the development of your world. It could be lost in the depths of one of the oceans, or deliberately dumped into a volcano. There's no way to know."

Haley was drawing patterns across his bare chest with her fingers, a move that was making it increasingly difficult to think straight. "And the other theory?" she asked.

"The ship didn't crash at all. It stayed in orbit while at least some of the colonists went down to the surface, likely to obtain raw materials for repairs or to acquire food or water. Our technology was far less sophisticated back then, and life on a colony ship was not easy. The second theory postulates that some of the colonists choose to stay and live among the humans. The ship and the rest of the colonists continued on their way, only to meet with catastrophe later on."

"The second theory sounds more likely to me." Haley gave him a sultry look that heated his blood. "We humans are very enticing."

"I don't know about other humans, but you, my *otama*, are enticingly beautiful and intelligent. Whatever you choose to do when we get to Pyros, I know you will be successful at it."

Her golden eyes gleamed with pleasure. "I think I know what I'm going to do. I'm going to write those articles I talked about, the ones that might help inform both our races about the other." She straightened up. "And then I'm going to write a book about it all."

It was a good idea, one that would counter some of the fear humans had about his race and their intentions. "Who better to write it than someone who had her own doubts and concerns? Later, I will introduce you to Prince Joran and his mate, Maggie. Once you have them convinced of the value of your plan, you should have no trouble getting all the resources and information you need."

She blinked at him. "You know the Prince and Princess well enough to ask that kind of favour?"

It belatedly occurred to him he had never actually told her his full job title. "I might not have mentioned it before, but the reason I am the Chief Medical Officer of the royal flagship is because I am responsible for the health of the royal family."

You really are an overachiever, aren't you?" she leaned in and kissed him. "That is for being so sweet and supportive of my idea."

He laughed and kissed her back. "And that is for making me think about my research differently. We make a good team."

"Yes, we do. It would appear the Gods knew what they were doing, after all."

He didn't bother to answer in words, but he made sure his feelings were clear to her through their link, which was now even stronger than before.

He picked up his tablet and started reading again, only to be interrupted a few seconds later.

"Tor, what the hell is that? I swear it looks like—" she pointed out the window.

"It appears the Romaki prince is on his way back to the ship. Interesting. I wasn't aware they were able to fly outside a planet's atmosphere. I'll have to ask him about that, it must have something to do with their magic."

"That's a dragon! I mean, I knew that's what he was, but… dragon!" Haley declared in shock.

"Well, yes. Did you not read the information I called up for you about his species?"

"No. I was busy reading through your stuff and jumping to conclusions," she reminded him.

"Ah, yes. You recognize the shape, though? Interesting. Vadir suspected humans had come across the Romaki before, based on your legends. Your reaction lends weight to his theory."

She leaned towards the window, her eyes widening yet again. "Is that a second dragon?"

Sure enough, there were two Romaki winging their way toward the ship, their massive bodies dwarfing the shuttlecraft following them. "It would appear so. It looks like your friend Aria is about to be reunited with her sister."

"Shit. She's not going to like this. That's her baby sister flapping her big, scaly wings out there." But he could feel her joy and delight flowing into him.

"You don't seem concerned."

"I'm not. Piper has been waiting for years to break away from her sister. Aria raised her when their mother died, and she has always been a bit overprotective." She gestured to the dragons and laughed. "She's a freaking dragon. Aria is going to have to let her go, now."

He wrapped his arms around her and held her close, marvelling again that this beautiful female was his. "Aria may let go of her sister, but I will never let go of you."

She leaned her head onto his shoulder and smiled. "You better not. You promised me we'd be together until we return to the flames that birthed us, remember? I'm hoping that day is a very long time from now."

"As do I, my love. As do I."

THE END

RADEK

Star-crossed Alien Mail Order Brides #6

What do you do when your friend's planet runs out of women? Join them for takeout, of course.

Radek is a prince with a problem. He wants to see the galaxy, but an ancient law forbids any member of the Romaki Dragon Clans from ever leaving their planet. So, what's a Romaki Snow Dragon to do? Defy the law, hop a ride with a friend, and head for the far side of the galaxy, that's what.

As the Pyrosians prepare to claim their mates, all Radek has to do is sit back, enjoy the party, and keep one little promise – no shifting into a dragon while he's visiting Earth. What could be simpler?

This book contains a sassy chef whose dreams just went up in flames, and a runaway prince who thought he was escaping his destiny…until she dropped right into his claws.

A SNEAK PEAK AT RADEK

Prince Radek Makyrn seethed with frustration, but he took care not to show it as he made his way through the crowd of revellers that filled the palace's largest ballroom. His parents were hosting a party in honour of their off-world guests, none of whom were aware that while they were enjoying themselves, their hosts had decided not to proceed with the trade talks. The Pyrosians had come all this way for nothing – again.

It took him a painfully long time to reach the edge of the crowd. Too many beings wanted a moment of his time. Some merely wanted to say hello, others flirted shamelessly, and the rest tried to use him as a messenger, hoping he would convey their wishes for meetings or favours to his mother. He politely greeted everyone, declined all flirtations, and deleted all the messages the moment he moved on. Even if he was inclined to help some of them, he knew it was a waste of time to try. During that last meeting his mother had proven yet again that she wouldn't listen to a word he said.

He was almost free when Savta found him, stepping into his path and placing her hand on his arm. "Good eve, Highness. Your mother sent me to find you."

Radek looked pointedly at her hand. "Did she also grant you permission to be so familiar with a member of the royal family?"

Savta moved her hand immediately. "She did not, though I am aware she wishes us to become much more familiar with each other, and soon."

"Are you also aware that I have not agreed to my mother's request, nor do I intend to?"

Savta tossed her long, dark hair back with a practiced gesture and laughed, but beneath the light, airy sound was an undertone of ice. "Be smart, Highness. If you refuse, she'll make it a royal command. I *will* be your consort. I promise, if you accept this fact gracefully, I will make sure you are well satisfied."

She didn't say more, but the threat was crystal clear. If he fought this, she'd make him regret it. He managed a broad smile. "Haven't you heard, Savta? I'm the foolish one in the family. I spend my days lost in writings about the past and contribute nothing to the present. Worse, I argue with the priests, my siblings, even my parents, whose word is law."

Her perfect features creased into a momentary frown. "You'd defy your mother's wishes?"

"She can order me to take you as my consort until I find my mate. She can even command me to move you into my rooms at the palace, but not even the ruler of my clan can control where I sleep, or with whom. You may sleep in my bed one day, but when that day comes, I will choose to sleep somewhere else."

"So be it. This could have been a pleasant and profitable interlude for us both while the search for our mates continues. Instead, you have chosen to insult and demean me. I won't forget this." She flounced off, no doubt to inform his mother what he'd done.

It was a good bet that by morning he'd either be in a cell or bound to that venomous *traxyn*. "I'm starting to think the Gods have it in for me," he muttered as he finally reached the outer doors, leaving the warmth and noise of the ballroom behind.

Out on the balcony, the night air was cold enough to turn his breath to vapour. It cut through his anger and frustration, helping him find a small measure of calm. It was just enough to stop him from giving in to his desire to launch himself into the air and shift to his dragon form and fly away. Not that there was anywhere he could go. He was too well known on his homeworld to stay hidden for long, and no member of his species was permitted to leave Romak.

Centuries ago, the Romaki had travelled the cosmos. They had colonized other worlds, trading with some species and warring with others. Then, the colonies had started failing, the survivors returning home defeated by weather, cataclysm, or war. More colony ships were sent out, only to vanish into the void. The priests claimed it was a sign of the Gods' displeasure, a warning that any Romaki that left the planet would invoke Sulan and Daga's wrath.

He stepped to the balustrade and leaned out to look at the palace grounds stretched out below, then raised his eyes to the star-filled sky. He didn't believe the priests. Everything he'd studied made him suspect it wasn't the Gods who wanted to keep his race bound to one planet, it was the priests who claimed to speak for them.

The doors opened again, releasing a blast of noise and light that filled the balcony and momentarily dimmed the stars. So much for his moment of peace.

He turned, then relaxed as he saw who it was – Vadir Rahal, one of the visiting Pyrosians. "Evening, Vadir."

"Highness." The dark-haired male replied in perfect Romaki and joined him at the railing. Vadir a highly profitable trading empire that spanned the length and breadth of known space. He'd been to Romak enough times that the two had become friends, a fact that had landed Radek in trouble with both the priests and his parents.

The two of them stared out at the stars for a while in companionable silence, but then Vadir asked a question Radek didn't expect. "When are they going to tell us the trade talks have been suspended?"

Radek turned, not bothering to hide his surprise. "How did you know?"

"I have my ways."

"Apparently. And to answer your question, I believe

the plan is to inform you and the rest of the delegation tomorrow morning. Did you get anything agreed to before they decided to end the talks?"

"Some. Mostly extending existing agreements." Vadir shrugged. "It's not what I hoped for."

"That seems to be a common sentiment around here today. The only ones who will be happy about this are the priests, may Sulan freeze their balls off."

"Talk like that is going to get you yet another lecture from the priests."

"They'll have to wait in line. I stood up to my mother tonight, trying to get her to see reason. We need more trade, not less. We're becoming a shadow of what we once were, afraid of anything different or new. It has to stop."

"Given that she cancelled the rest of the talks, I'm going to guess she didn't agree with you."

Radek smacked a hand down on the railing. "She did not. She thinks I need to stop studying the past and make more of an effort to represent the family in the present."

"She's finally decided to give you some responsibility, then?"

"Hardly," Radek scoffed. "She wants me to take a consort until such time as one of us finds our mate."

"Who?"

"Savta."

Vadir curled his lip with distaste. "My condolences. Is there any way you can avoid this arrangement without angering your parents even more? I can't see you being happy with someone with Savta's temperament."

Radek laughed. "Too late. Savta and I had words on my way out here. I told her it would take a royal command before I'd accept her as my consort. I have no doubt my mother has already heard about it."

"And while you wait for your punishment, you're sitting out here, contemplating the stars." Vadir looked up. "Do you ever wish you could go out there and see the galaxy for yourself?"

"Every day," he admitted.

"You know, my mate is from a planet on the far side of the galaxy. We're going to be heading there once we leave Romak."

Curious to see where Vadir was going with this, he played along. "Earth, right? I had the pleasure of speaking with Lisa earlier today. She's looking forward to returning home for a visit. It sounds like an interesting place."

"Did she happen to mention that her species have legends about a mythical scaled creature that breathed fire and flew?"

"Many species have myths about monsters and creatures that never existed." He was trying to play it cool, but his interest was piqued.

"Mhmm," Vadir drawled. "Any of them have a word in their language for dragon?"

"What? Really?"

Vadir nodded, his smile broadening. "Really. As far

as I can tell, it appears that the Pyrosians weren't the only aliens to spend some time on Earth."

"Do you have proof of this? If you did, it could change everything! The priests claim that Romaki that leaves the planet is punished by the Gods and stripped of their magic. If there were Romaki on Earth in their dragon form, that proves they're wrong."

"I don't have proof, no. That's back on Earth." He paused for half a heartbeat before adding. "If you came with us, you could find the proof you need yourself."

"Came with you, to Earth? Leave Romak?" Radek was still trying to absorb Vadir's news. His brain wasn't ready to process an invitation to fulfill his greatest wish and visit another planet.

"That's exactly what I mean. Unless you'd rather stay here and take your chances with Savta?"

The reminder made his decision easy. "By Solun's frosty beard, no. If I go with you, all I'm risking is the wrath of the Gods and the potential loss of my magic. That's preferable to staying here with my mother and Savta."

Vadir clapped a hand to his shoulder. "I thought so."

"You realize if my parents figure out where I am and who I am with, it's not going to go well for you or any future trade talks?" He knew Vadir had already done a careful study of the risks versus potential rewards before he decided to make the offer, but he still felt it needed to be said.

"True. But if you come back with verifiable evidence the priests are wrong, think of all the opportunities that open up." Vadir spread his hands wide. "Increased trade. Renewed travel. Shipbuilding."

"And since you'll be the first to know what I find, you'll have the advantage?"

"Exactly. I'm going to make a businessman out of you, yet, Highness."

"Good. If this doesn't work out the way you hope, I'll be asking you for a job." He'd need one, too, because if he did this, the temples would declare him outcast and he'd never be allowed to return home.

Vadir nodded, his expression serious for once. "I've got your back, but I'm confident you're not going to need my help."

"You can't be sure."

"I am. I can't tell you why, though. Ask me about it when we're on our way home from Earth."

"Believe me, I will. Which brings me to my next questions – how do you plan on getting me off the planet?"

"That's easy enough. Tonight, I'm going to take you, and several other VIP's on a tour of my ship. When the group leaves, you'll stay behind. Once we get official word the talks are suspended, Lisa and I will express our displeasure, return to the ship within the hour, and depart with my usual dramatic flair. We'll be halfway across the galaxy before anyone knows you're gone."

Radek nodded as a plan started to come together in his mind. "That will work. I'll leave a message behind, something to lead everyone to believe I left to avoid Savta and my mother but will be back in a few days.

I've done it before. If I leave a few items with you tonight, can you bring them aboard with your own things?"

"Of course," Vadir confirmed.

He looked around the grounds of the palace one last time. He'd grown up here, exploring every inch of the grounds. He'd learned to shift his form out in the wide stretch of lawn, practiced controlling his magic by freezing the fountains, and created a small crater in a distant corner while he was still mastering takeoffs and landings. If Vadir was wrong, this might be the last time he looked out at this view. He fixed it in his memory, then turned his back on the garden, and all the memories it held. "Then I better start packing.

"Shit!" Piper slammed her cell phone down on the table harder than she intended. There was a cracking sound, and when she picked it up again, the screen had a spectacular web of cracks in the center. "Double shit. This day better not get any worse."

She could deal with a busted cell phone. She wasn't coping as well with the news she'd just lost a job she hadn't even started yet, but she'd get that handled. It's not like she'd been fired. The restaurant had burned down before it even opened, and the owner had promised that once they got the insurance figured out they'd rebuild, and her job would be waiting for her. She'd find a way to get by until then, she always did.

She just didn't want anything else to go wrong, because today was important to her older sister, Aria. Ri was going to meet her match from the Star-Crossed Dating Agency, and Piper was hoping that today was the day her sister found some happiness. Even if that happiness came in the form of a hot guy from another planet.

"This is now officially a double shot of espresso kind of morning." She set the phone down, carefully this time, and went to the kitchen in search of caffeine. After that phone call, she might even break out the whipped cream and vanilla syrup.

The mug was almost empty by the time she started feeling better. She'd done some math, checked her bank balance, and sent out emails to a few contacts to let them know she was looking for employment, again. She'd also decided not to tell Aria about the fire. Her sister was already determined to turn down the match and retreat back into her safe, lonely life as a single mom. If she found out that Piper's dream job had literally gone up in smoke, she'd use it as an excuse to stay home instead of meeting her match in person. Piper was determined to get Aria to the Gathering at BC Place Stadium. Maybe if she met this guy in person, she'd change her mind about turning him down.

Piper had joined the same dating agency, but so far there was no match for her in their database. Unlike Ri, if she ever got matched, she'd be ready to take off for another planet in a heartbeat. It would be the adventure of a lifetime. She could already see herself opening a restaurant on Pyros, offering Earth-style meals to an entire planet full of eager customers. Not to mention that fact that being on the other side of the galaxy might just put enough distance between her and Ri to let her live her own life.

Their mother had died when she was still a teenager, and Aria had stepped into the role of mother-figure and guardian, while Piper had dealt with her grief by rebelling against anyone and anything she could think of. She'd outgrown that phase years ago, but not before it laid out the template of their adult relationship. It didn't help that she'd moved back in after Aria had her baby. She adored Hope and was happy to help, but the second Piper moved home again, they'd fallen into old habits.

"And now I'm moping like a teenager. Next thing you know I'll be digging out my black lipstick and writing bad poetry." She drained her mug and headed for the bedroom. It was time to get ready for the Gathering. She'd already picked the perfect outfit, a cute blue and white mini-dress that happened to be a perfect match for her freshly dyed hair. She might not be one of the lucky matches, but she planned on looking good and enjoying herself anyway. If nothing else, five hundred hot aliens ready to meet their matches should make for a hell of a view.

Several hours later, she and her sister's best friend, Haley, had claimed their seats and spotted Aria among the women nervously waiting to meet their matches. The stadium roof was open, letting the summer sunshine pour in. The organizers had set up a beautiful open-sided white tent decorated with lavish displays of flowers. The women were all seated beneath it, chattering to each other as they tried to subtly sneak looks at the stage and the men standing around it. Judging by their matching uniforms and serious expressions they had to be the Pyrosians, but apart from their larger builds, they looked human enough.

Movement on the near side of the stage caught her attention. She watched with interest as two men, both wearing what had to be hand-tailored suits, appeared. They were followed by several more of the uniformed aliens, who seemed to be acting as bodyguards. They must be VIPs. They were both good-looking, one dark-haired, the other so blonde his hair looked almost white. It was the blonde that kept her attention. He kept looking around the stadium, his expression one of intense interest. A blonde woman in a bright orange and yellow sundress joined the men, and Piper exhaled in relief when she greeted the dark-haired one with a kiss, but only smiled at blondie. *Because it's totally rational to feel possessive about a total stranger.*

Once she got over her irrational response and focused on the woman, she realized she recognized her. "Is that one of the women from the ads?" Piper asked Haley.

"I think so, yeah. So that guy she just smooched must be her mate."

Haley started snapping pictures with her phone. Later, Piper planned to ask her for some of them since she couldn't take any herself. Not with her phone in its current condition. More people started arriving, all of them smartly dressed and accompanied by a camera crew. They exchanged greetings and handshakes with the two men she'd been watching, and then all of them headed for their seats in a roped off area beside the stage.

Down on the stadium floor, the women waited for their matches with growing nervousness, and around the stage there was a flurry of activity.

She didn't even notice the space shuttle descending into the arena until everyone around her started to gasp and point upward. At the same time, several columns of identically dressed men marched into sight. They were all staring at the women seated beneath the tent, and even from this distance, there was no mistaking their eager, hopeful expressions. One day, she wanted a guy to look at *her* that way.

Even as that crossed her mind, she looked away from the spectacle to scan the VIP seating. The handsome blond she'd been crushing on was watching the shuttle approach, but after a second, his gaze shifted and she could almost swear he was looking back at her. Before she could be sure, though, the stadium erupted into a cacophony of flames, fire, and screams.

Order Radek Now

Want to read more stories with book boyfriends
that are out of this world?

**Check out Susan Hayes' other Science Fiction
Romance Titles**

<u>The Drift</u>
Double Down
All In
Wild Card
Three of a Kind
No Limit
Blind Bet
Aces Over Queen

<u>Nova Force</u>
Operation Phoenix
Operation Cobalt

<u>3013: The Series</u>
3013: RENEGADE
3013: STOWAWAY
3013: TARGETED
3013: FATED
3013: SCARRED

Susan lives out on the Canadian west coast surrounded by open water, dear family, and good friends. She's jumped out of perfectly good airplanes on purpose and accidentally swum with sharks on the Great Barrier Reef.

If the world ends, she plans to survive as the spunky, comedic sidekick to the heroes of the new world, because she's too damned short and out of shape to make it on her own for long.

You can find out more about Susan and her books here:
www.susanhayes.ca

www.ingramcontent.com/pod-product-compliance
Lightning Source LLC
Chambersburg PA
CBHW021731190726
48288CB00009B/2995